TRANSPLANT

Wayne took a few steps towards her, stopped and said, "I've noticed you."

"Oh? Why?"

"Because. . ." He hesitated. "Because you're not grey."

"You really mean, because of my face."

"Suppose," he muttered. "You can't miss it, like."

That was it. Cassie shrank back into her own shell. She guessed that he meant no harm. He was just stating an undeniable fact. And after all, she'd prompted his display of straight talking. But she hadn't yet had a chance to get accustomed to blunt honesty. Perhaps she wouldn't have to – if she had her transplant soon. Then, she'd have to get accustomed to wearing a dead girl's face instead.

Point

TRANSPLANT

MALCOLM ROSE

■SCHOLASTIC

Scholastic Children's Books,
Commonwealth House, 1-19 New Oxford Street,
London, WC1A 1NU, UK
A division of Scholastic Ltd
London ~ New York ~ Toronto ~ Sydney ~ Auckland
Mexico City ~ New Delhi ~ Hong Kong

First published in the UK by Scholastic Ltd, 2003

Copyright © Malcolm Rose, 2003

ISBN 0 439 98205 7

All rights reserved

Printed and bound in Great Britain by Cox & Wyman Ltd, Reading, Berkshire

1 2 3 4 5 6 7 8 9 10

The right of Malcolm Rose to be identified as the author of this work has been asserted by him
in accordance with the Copyright, Designs and Patents Act, 1988.

With particular thanks to
Emah Mardlin
Dennis Robinson

The idea of taking off a dead person's face and putting it on someone else appears to have come straight out of science fiction. However, recipient patients have serious physical and psychological problems that cannot be solved by conventional treatments. If face transplantation is shown to be the only effective way of treating these severely disfigured patients, then doctors would have a duty to use the technique.

Shehan Hettiaratchy and Peter E M Butler, Transplantation Biology Research Center, Massachusetts General Hospital and Department of Plastic Surgery, Royal Free Hospital, London. In The Lancet, July 6, 2002.

ACID 1

The milk bottle flew over the helmets of the riot squad, over their armoured Land Rovers and horses, and plunged down on Cassie. She screamed and clutched at her forehead. It wasn't the shock or the pain. On her way to school, Cassie had grown used to the sticks and stones and, even worse, the awful words of the angry mob of Protestants behind the police line. No, it was another thought that made her shriek. Immediately, her mind turned to Bernadette. Her old friend had been showered with petrol and set on fire in this godforsaken place. Cassie had never found out why. Maybe a Protestant gang had attacked her, not because of her race, not because she worshipped the wrong god, but because of the way she worshipped God. Or maybe Catholic extremists had assaulted her, not because Bernie had done something wicked, but because she had information they wanted.

But the clear liquid trickling over Cassie's mousy hair, her hands and down her face did not reek of fuel. Her fingers were not soaked in petrol. They didn't smell of anything. For a moment, she felt relieved and merely bruised by the missile. Curious, she looked at her hands in the instant before her eyes closed involuntarily. Her palms had turned a peculiar shade of yellow and they stung as if they were on fire. The same burning sensation enveloped the top of her head and face. Now there was a smell but it wasn't the liquid. It was the appalling stench of smouldering flesh even though there were no flames. Cassie shivered as she realized that something was dreadfully, horribly wrong. And then the liquid flowed into her eyes and mouth, smarting and blistering instantly. Overcome by agony, she screamed again. Her howl silenced the crowd with its intensity.

Cassie didn't understand that she'd been hit by Belfast's first acid bomb.

Noises: bleeps, footsteps and cries. Glimpses: ghostly characters in gowns, hazy ceilings moving past. When her eyes weren't covered with a dressing, her vision was curiously restricted and flat, like looking at a TV screen rather than real life. And a badly tuned TV at that. Medication: injections and tablets. Voices: Irish, English and Asian accents expressing anger, distress, concern, hope. The least of these seemed to be hope. At one point, Cassie believed she even heard the unusual sound of her father's voice. She also heard someone swearing, slurring as if drunk, using words that a Catholic girl would never use, so she was amazed to realize that she was the one who was mouthing them. Smell: overpowering disinfectant. Sensations: rough linen and hands squeezing her arm as if trying desperately to reassure. When she summoned the strength to move her fingers, she felt a smooth rustling. There was an indistinct pain, nausea and an insatiable irritation around her face and hands. Every time she blinked, her eyelid scraped across the surface of her eye as if she had something scratchy adhering permanently to it. The feeling frustrated and infuriated her.

Her life had become a jigsaw. She could take in only a few fragments at a time and they barely made sense. She certainly couldn't fit them together to make a coherent picture any more.

"Cassie, love. I'm so sorry. I'll see you as much as I can but it won't be for a while. It's for your own good because things have got a bit hot. I'll be thinking about you, though."

Cassie hated what her father had done to their family. She heard his words, heard the sorrow in his voice, but she wasn't sure if she'd really seen him at her bedside, surrounded by plain-clothed security men as always. Maybe she'd just imagined the scene.

There was a face, invading her personal space, peering closely at her. Then there was a blinding light in her right eye.

A male Asian voice sounded serious and sympathetic like a doctor. "There's a problem grafting skin from her leg. Even after multiple operations, she won't look natural because you can't make another part of the body look like a face. And there'll be unsightly scar tissue. But there's an alternative. I could refer her to a specialist unit in England for treatment. It's still experimental though. . ."

Tubes. She was aware of a lot of tubes. Whichever way she turned in her bed, she yanked on one. It made her feel like a machine, plugged into the mains. She hardly dared to move for fear of severing her power supply.

"Reporters? Wanting her story? What do they think this is: a soap opera? No chance."

She remembered one thing very clearly: a total lack of mirrors. She wasn't sure if that was by accident or design but she feared the worst.

MARBLE 2

By the time that Cassie began to understand the world again – and understand what had happened to her – she was in a high-dependency ward of the Department of Experimental Medicine in Sheffield. The unit was a cross between a hospital and a university research wing and it stepped in when conventional medicine failed. Like a plucked chicken wrapped in a supermarket, Cassie's ravaged face was packaged in a tight transparent plastic mask. Even her hands were tied up in plastic bags.

The surgeon drew up a chair beside Cassie's bed, as if sitting on the edge of the bed itself was too intimate. Dr Staunton needed to keep an official distance between them. "How are you doing, Cassandra?"

Because of her narrow field of view, Cassie had to turn her whole head towards the source of the sound. She couldn't seem to swivel her eyes so she had to endure the pain of twisting her neck. Once she'd got the doctor in focus, she had a curious sensation of detachment, an inability to judge the distance between them. "I just want to be normal again." Cassie wanted to sound indignant, frustrated, angry, but her facial injuries prevented her from venting her feelings. Poorly pronounced words merely dribbled out of her misshapen mouth. It took an enormous effort to utter anything at all. Expressing emotion was out of the question.

"Normal's not going to be easy, Cassandra."

"Cassie." She hated it when people assumed that her name was short for Cassandra and now she hated the way her mouth could manage only "Cashie". She wished she'd chosen a different name altogether. "I want to be up and about. I want my friends and school. I want to use a mirror and make-up." It was painful to speak. Every movement seemed to tug on her already taut lips.

Dr Staunton nodded. "I know. But you've got more important things to take care of first. I can help, but it'll take time."

"How do you mean?"

"Well, you're coming up to a big decision. I've had a good look at your details, I've examined you thoroughly, and you'd be able to try a new treatment – if you want to."

Cassie's face might be in disarray but her brain was as sharp as ever. "What's the catch?" she said in her distorted splutter.

Dr Staunton shuffled uncomfortably in her chair. "Let's just think about where we are, before we decide where we want to go. Your face and hands have been attacked by acid, Cassie. I'm sorry. You've been told that part of your nose and mouth have come away. The rest is going to be badly scarred. You've lost your eyebrows, eyelashes and your left eyelid. It didn't protect you as it should so I'm afraid you've lost that eye. It's so damaged, we'll have to remove it in due course. Your right eyelid did better and you've still got sight there."

Yes, she'd been told but, without seeing, she could not take it in. "I want to see."

"You have a face in transition, Cassie. It's not how it was and it's not how you'll look after treatment."

"I still want to see." Cassie was really annoyed with the lisping sound coming out of her mouth. It reminded her of someone struggling to speak after being anaesthetized at the dentist.

"There are no mirrors in this ward, Cassie. That's the policy."

Straining her neck to glance around, Cassie saw only bright and bubbly paintings decorating the department, blurred by her fragile vision.

"Why?"

Dr Staunton took a deep breath. "Because it'd be wrong to base a patient's treatment on their first reaction to seeing their appearance. We don't want rash decisions. I don't want anyone to say I took advantage and forced a new procedure on someone when they were at their lowest ebb."

"What new procedure?" asked Cassie.

"You have to be realistic over what we can achieve with normal surgery. It's good but it's long-winded and the results are. . ." She shrugged. "Not as attractive as we'd wish. We can do something about the pain after skin-graft operations but we can't make a perfect repair. Don't get me wrong. You could still have a full and rewarding life. In all honesty, though, I couldn't call it normal. There's worse things than facial disfigurement but other people have a problem with it. I'm afraid they either stare or look away. I want to put a stop to all that. I think I can. I've pioneered a new technique but it's not routine yet."

"What is it?"

"We could do a transplant," Dr Staunton said.

To Cassie, the surgeon's comment didn't make sense. Of course she knew about heart transplants, liver, kidney and lung transplants, and she thought bone-marrow and maybe other organs could be transplanted, but she'd been led to believe that she didn't have anything wrong internally. She couldn't make her face form a baffled expression so she muttered, "I don't follow. What's wrong with me?"

Dr Staunton smiled, leaned forward and clasped her arm reassuringly. "It's OK. It was always going to be a shock. I mean a face transplant."

Without eyebrows, Cassie could not express astonishment either. "What?"

"That's the decision, Cassie. To go with conventional surgery or to try for a brand new perfect face."

"But. . ." Cassie had far more questions than she had words available to her damaged mouth. How could they get another face? Who would it belong to? How could they put it on her? What would happen if it went wrong? What – or who – would she look like?

Dr Staunton nodded. "I know what's on your mind. It's all too much right now, too many answers you'd need. We'll talk later but for the moment just think about it. I can give you a transplant – much faster and less painful than all those skin grafts, and with far better results – but it's cutting-edge medicine. You'd be the first subject."

Cassie stared with her one eye, unable to respond. She felt sick, deep in her stomach. She shivered at the thought of someone else's face, a dead person's flesh, fixed on to her bones. It wouldn't be like having someone else's heart or even their hand – she could cope with either of those transplants. But a face! A face was so . . . personal, so visible.

The doctor stood up and stretched her back. "It's important to realize that I'm not putting any pressure on you, Cassie, but you'd have a cosmetically perfect face rather than a patchwork repair."

With that dreadful slushy sound, Cassie strained to say, "It's gross."

"It'd be wrong to make a rash decision either way."

"I've got to see what I look like."

"You've got to judge the transplant against what we could do with plastic surgery. You can't see that in a mirror. The best I can do is arrange for you to see someone who's had conventional skin grafts – a girl called Taslima who had acid thrown in her face as well."

Overwhelmed, Cassie sighed hopelessly. "I have to go to the toilet."

"I'll call a nurse." Dr Staunton hesitated for a moment. She seemed to make up her mind and added, "Perhaps it's time you got a bit more mobile. See if you can manage in a proper toilet. That'd be good, wouldn't it? There's someone in this bathroom but I can get a nurse to uncouple you from everything – just for a bit – and wheel you to the next-door ward. OK?"

Cassie's faint nod was the best she could manage.

From a moving wheelchair, Cassie could not see well. Her eyesight wasn't brilliant any more but, even so, she got the impression that all of the patients were not just adult but old. She seemed to be the youngest in the mixed-sex unit.

When the nurse halted by a desk to talk briefly to a colleague, Cassie was able to focus much better. A middle-aged woman sitting on a chair beside her bed was decidedly yellow. Next to her, an elderly man with a peculiar dressing on the side of his head was clearly blind. Oddest of all, an even older man had a neck that appeared to be transparent. The see-through skin provided a macabre window on his blood vessels, muscle and throat. He had adorned the area around his bed with model aeroplanes. The planes were old and small, green and grey. Cassie guessed that they were models of the aircraft used in World War II. The man was sitting up in bed, hunched over another model, very carefully gluing a wing on to a fuselage. Cassie got the impression he was a devoted and meticulous craftsman.

Turning her neck gingerly, Cassie saw a nurse removing one of the paintings and replacing it with an even more vivid piece featuring sailing boats. Closer, a female flamenco dancer in a layered purple dress and a flamboyant man with an acoustic guitar filed past her. Cassie was amazed that anyone would visit a hospital dressed like that.

It also struck Cassie as strange that the patients were so varied. She expected a row of the same sort of complaints: all burns victims or broken bones or cancer cases. Collecting together sundry conditions was an odd way for the Department of Experimental Medicine to specialize, she thought. She couldn't dwell on it, though, because the nurse was pushing her again. The double doors crashed open and Cassie was into the neighbouring ward, straight up to the toilet door.

As soon as Cassie staggered into the bathroom, she

understood. Dr Staunton had dutifully followed the unit's policy but she was also taking pity on her patient. Sometime, Cassie had to confront her injuries and obviously Dr Staunton believed that the time was right. The surgeon would have known that, in this ward, there was a mirror attached to the bathroom wall.

Unexpectedly confronted by a face in that mirror, Cassie couldn't accept that it was hers. "It can't be!" she screamed internally, her heart suddenly pounding. She looked behind her but she knew there was no one else in the room. That awful image had to be her. She grabbed the edge of the sink with her fists but immediately let go because of the tenderness of her hands.

Gathering her strength, she forced herself to peer into the glass again. Uncomfortably close, the puffy face looked as if it had been sandpapered. It was smooth like moulded plastic, raw red and totally hairless. The whole thing was a cruel mask or a face-painting for someone about to star in a horror film as a grotesque breed of vampire. A face like that would frighten anyone. It scared the wits out of Cassie.

Her hairline was way back on her head. Her brow looked as if she'd just headed an incredibly muddy football. Her left eye was an opaque orb. Even her good eye was inflamed, with a scrappy flap of skin as an excuse for an eyelid. Her nose was a complete mess and one nostril had disappeared altogether. It was a lopsided splodge that had no right to be attached to anyone's face. Under the remains of her nose was a darker stain, running above her lips, round her mouth and down on to her chin. Plainly, the brown moustache marked acid tracks.

11

No wonder she couldn't speak well. Her lips, where they had not melted away, were enlarged, bright red and shiny. In one corner, though, they were missing. Her teeth and gums were showing. Yes, she'd have provided a wonderfully scary moment in a horror film. From now on, that's what she'd be: a ghoul in the entertainment business.

Staring into that mirror, one other thing surprised her. Despite the damage to her eyes, her tear ducts were still working fine. Tears flowed even from the blank marble.

TESTOSTERONE  3

Hilary Staunton felt like an intruder in an all-male club. Even though she lacked the most essential equipment for a leading medic – a body brimming with testosterone – she was better than the other team leaders. Her research into new transplant techniques was way ahead of the department's other programmes.

Jealous of her success and annoyed by her gender, her fellow medics did their best to criticize her work. In response, she had become skilled in defending her methods and she enjoyed crushing their criticism. She was frustrated that a lingering prejudice stopped her storming through the medical ranks but she wouldn't let it impede her work. Ruthlessness and the drive to succeed came naturally to her.

Hilary struck a rather masculine pose, mug in hand, slouched in a seat, feet up on the one in front. Trying to keep a smirk from her face, she was listening to her testosterone-laden colleagues giving brief talks on their latest work. The members of the Department of Experimental Medicine could afford the luxury of a weekly research break because they were part of the university and not simply components of the hospital machine. They weren't forced to dash around, relentlessly shell-shocked, at the whim of the National Health Service. Over several mugs of thick coffee, the six team leaders – all promoted to professor apart from herself – were outlining progress in their own fields. Brain implants aimed at giving vision to the blind, stem cells to grow new body parts, the role of art and music in therapy, making skin temporarily transparent to simplify skin cancer surgery, tiny robots that could be injected into the body to repair ailments as they arose. Only Richard Clayton, with his nanorobots, was keeping pace with Hilary's strides in transplant surgery.

When it was her turn to update the department, she relished her ability to make even hardened medics squirm. She reported that she could now transplant faces because her new immunosuppressant drug stopped patients rejecting all sorts of foreign tissue, even skin. At least, in theory. "You all know it's a major triumph to develop medication that'll stop skin from being rejected by a host. And because the anti-rejection drug works with skin, it'll probably work with any tissue. I'm getting some organs grown in animals for transplant into suitable human recipients. I've got a female patient waiting for a kidney from a transgenic pig. Anyway, the pills open all sorts of doors and, as you know, I'm particularly keen to repair disfigured faces. I'm ready to lift a face, complete with muscles, nerves, eyelids and lips, from a cadaver and lay it down on the existing bony scaffolding of any face severely damaged by fire, dog attack, acid, traffic accident, bullet wounds or disease. If the underlying bone's damaged as well, I can repair it by grafting some bone from the donor at the same time.

"And there's something else. Blood vessels aren't a big problem. The carotid artery supplies the face with blood bilaterally and the jugular vein drains it, also bilaterally. They're a doddle to connect up. No. Along with rejection, the other major challenge is nerve regeneration to give the recipient feeling and expression, to make the face work. I can align and join the facial and trigeminal nerves but the patient's neurons have got to regrow into the transplanted nerves. That's been a stumbling block, but not now. My immunosuppressant drug acts like a growth factor, accelerating nerve repair."

When she'd finished her talk, she faced the questions.

"Your drug might speed up nerve regeneration but all anti-rejection treatments slow down the healing of wounds. After surgery, you're going to get seriously infected wounds."

Hilary dismissed the claim. "That's the beauty of my drug. It's selective. It suppresses the immune system so it doesn't reject foreign tissue but it doesn't wipe out the body's natural defence against infection. It's reduced, I'll give you that, but no more."

"You'll still need elaborate precautions for surgery."

"I've drawn up a perfectly workable plan."

"Has anyone tried face transplant operations on animals?"

Hilary shook her head. "Vets don't have my microsurgery skills and no one's got an anti-rejection drug for animals." She hesitated before deciding on a light-hearted approach. "Besides, vets'd rather I experiment on humans first, before they risk animals and the wrath of pet owners."

Ignoring her joke, Richard asked, "How are you going to make sure you're selecting the right patient? It raises all sorts of ethical issues."

"And nanomedicine doesn't?"

To get his own back, Richard said, "I go to great lengths to stay on the right side of ethics. No patient's pressurized by me."

There was an implication that they thought Hilary was pushing her methods too hard and too early at vulnerable patients. Well, she'd had to learn how to be a fighter. She'd always had to fight harder and smarter than them, to land an occasional punch below the belt. She was fighting to penetrate their male stronghold, to secure funds for her work, to get her transplant methods accepted. And she was fighting the Ethics Committee for her right to improve patients' lives. "Come on. You all know a heart transplant once raised everyone's hackles. Now it's mainstream and perfectly safe. Face transplants might make people feel queasy right now but they'll happen and when patients come out looking great they'll adjust. Remember, the department's slogan is *Rebuilding Lives*. You see it every day written over the entrance. That's exactly what I'm doing. Every time someone suffers a catastrophic injury, I'm the one they'll turn to. I'll soon be able to patch anything. But I don't trample all over patients to do it. *They'll* decide, not me."

"This acid-attack girl, Cassandra—"

"Cassie," Hilary said.

"You're lining her up for the first face transplant, it's clear."

"*If* that's what she wants."

"Who's the donor? Have you lined that up as well?"

"A suitable donor'll be hard to find, I admit,"

Dr Staunton answered. "I'll have to match skin colour, age, blood type and immunological profile."

"Do you really think relatives of the dead are going to be happy to have their loved ones used like this? It's . . . undignified to say the least."

Hilary replied, "Plenty of people die anonymously and without known relatives. Some illegal immigrants and homeless, for instance. But plenty of people leave their bodies to science as well. On top of that, if enough money's on offer, some relatives would be tempted. There won't be a queue, but I'll get donors."

One of her colleagues screwed his face up into a sanctimonious scowl. He was thinking of unsavoury wrangles over dead bodies. "Wouldn't the recipient be picky over the appearance of a donor's face? I know I would."

"Next week, I'm seeing a man who's had a tumour the size of a tennis ball removed from his face. I don't know how picky you'd be if that was you. But, yes, you're right. Even with a face reduced to pulp, they might be choosy. It's not a race, though. The right donor'll come along sooner or later."

"There's no room for error here, is there? It's a horrid thought that the drug might fail and a patient reject their nice new face."

Hilary dismissed the question. "It works," she stated bluntly and with absolute confidence.

Another medic claimed, "Tissue engineering'll make a lot of this transplant technology unnecessary. I'll be able to regrow damaged skin using the patient's own stem cells so rejection won't be an issue."

Hilary snorted. "Note the future tense. You haven't grown a fully functioning mouse kidney yet, never mind anything more complex. Tissue engineering's years away. Ninety per cent of my patients would be dead by then."

"You'll need a counsellor to help people who come round after surgery with someone else's face or pig organs. That's going to take some dealing with."

"Fine," Hilary said. "Then I'll employ a counsellor."

"Yes, your funds are well topped up at the moment. But I don't like the look of your sponsors. All those rich celebrities who're getting on a bit. I can see their motives and I don't like the direction they'll push you in."

"Jealous, eh?" Hilary replied sharply. "They're just a means to an end. Think instead about the accident victims, the terrible scarring." Her envious colleagues might have professorial pay packets but her work attracted the most sponsors. Hilary didn't like appealing for funds – it was the worst part of her job – but it was necessary and she was good at it.

"Is it because of your ageing pop stars and the like that we've acquired a permanent bodyguard at the entrance – under the *Rebuilding Lives* logo?"

"Sorry about that. It's Cassie. She's got a family history. I haven't been told what exactly but it means she's got to be protected. He's here for the duration of her treatment, I'm afraid. Nothing to do with celebrities."

Self-righteous as always, Richard put up his hand with forefinger and thumb nearly touching. "You're this far from cosmetic surgery, Hilary."

"Cassie won't care what you call it. She just wants a

normal life." Hilary leaned forward and let rip. "You go out there and tell her we're not going to help because it's too close to cosmetic surgery. And while you're at it, tell soldiers not to get their faces blown off in wars, tell people travelling in cars, trains and planes to dodge the flames if they're involved in a crash, and tell cancer patients not to let rampant tumours eat away half their faces. If that's fine with you, I'll stop the research."

Hilary's point hit home and the other team leaders finally fell silent.

"No more questions?" she said, gathering up her notes. "Good. I'm off to get some work done."

4 INSULIN

The two police officers looked through the hole, no bigger than a letter box. "What do you think?" the constable asked the duty sergeant. "He said he'd been sick when I brought him in. Then he claimed he was dizzy and thirsty, full of headache. He guzzled a lot of water, keeled over and just lay there."

"He's been bingeing or having you on."

"He'd didn't smell of drink. More . . . I don't know . . . fruity than alcohol."

"He's play-acting then."

The PC nodded in agreement. "Wayne!" he shouted into the cell. "Stop pissing about, son. It won't do you any good."

The boy, as thin as a stick, was stretched out on the rough bunk. No movement, not even a suppressed giggle.

The duty sergeant sighed. "Well, you know the routine."

"But he's just messing us about."

"Yeah, but if there's really something wrong with him, you'll find yourself in front of the boss explaining why you didn't pull the doctor in. Shortly after, you'll find yourself in the queue at the Job Centre."

"But. . ."

"Play by the book. Call the doctor."

The constable groaned. "I thought I was supposed to be

out there catching crooks, not in here filing forms, mollycoddling rogues like him."

"All part of life's rich tapestry. Go on. Do your duty." He inclined his head towards the door of the cell and added, "His health may not depend on it but your salary does."

Both of them were wrong. Wayne Wingate was dying slowly in custody. His blood was jam-packed with glucose, his urine was brimming with sugar and poisonous ketone bodies, his blood pressure was soaring. The police doctor diagnosed severe acidosis, verging on coma, due to diabetes. Wayne's body had gone into shock and his heart was stressed. At once, the doctor administered a massive dose of insulin and called the hospital.

5 GLUCOSE

The hospital stuck a drip into Wayne's hand and woke him
every hour to prick a fingertip and test his blood for glucose.
Within three days, his blood sugar had been stabilized and
he was eating normally. And he'd had countless, tedious
lectures from Dr Flint about diabetes, insulin, diet, exercise
and, above all else, routine. Wayne had also had injection
lessons. Jabs didn't bother him. Sliding the needle into the
flesh of his stomach was no problem. Pricking his finger
and doing the blood test was no problem. Low fat, low sugar,
high exercise was no problem. What bothered him was
organizing a routine. Wayne's lifestyle wasn't ideally suited
to organization and routine.

He lived with his uncle and auntie – most of the time.
The rest, he lived with mates, in a squat, all over the place.
His uncle and aunt didn't really want him and didn't have
enough room for him either. His real mother had
abandoned him when he was still a baby and her brother
had picked up the pieces. The pretend-dad had given
Wayne a home out of shame, nothing to do with love and
caring.

Dr Flint stood with Wayne in the ward and said, "The
police told me you're a bit of a lad. What did they mean?"

Head bowed, Wayne muttered, "Dunno."

"Are you at school?"

"Sometimes."

"Sometimes?"

"They don't teach you nothing useful."

"I see. And you live with relatives some of the time. So, I suppose we're saying you're not best placed to get into the habit of insulin injections."

"Suppose."

"And what do you do for money?"

"This and that."

"You mean scrounging and stealing."

For once, Wayne looked into Dr Flint's face but he didn't say anything.

"That's what the police told me. Don't think I'm getting at you, Wayne. I'm not here to judge you. I'm just here to keep you alive, out of danger and out of hospital. To do that, I need to know what sort of life you lead. Then, I can give you the treatment and advice that suits you best."

"I like it here, me. Right good food." Wayne had got friendly with lots of nurses, and they really cared about him. He didn't want to leave the hospital.

"Yes, you get a bed and a roof over your head as well but we can't afford to be your hotel. Besides, it's not home. That's where you get emotional support. You'd keep your diabetes under best control with four regular injections a day but I'm guessing that's going to be tricky for you so I'm considering one big dose a day. What do you think?"

Wayne merely shrugged.

"We'll give it a go, with a weekly visit to the diabetes specialist nurse. If it doesn't keep you off the ward, we'll have to think again."

"I'm not gonna let this thing rule my life."

The stethoscope round Dr Flint's neck looked like a loose dog collar. It suited him because he preached endlessly to diabetics. "No, it won't do that. Giving yourself injections and testing your blood, it's like brushing your teeth. If you build it into your routine, it's easy."

"You said I got to eat regular. My folks have got to know where I am all the time, my mates have got to know what to do if I collapse again. I've got to have insulin, food and cash with me all the time. That's not easy."

"Being sixteen, you might not get a disability living allowance. You're a bit old but, you never know, you should give it a go. You might get it on appeal. Fifty quid a week would help, wouldn't it?"

"Suppose." Wayne didn't trust free handouts and he certainly wasn't going to crawl in front of some appeals panel, full of posh people who'd hate him. He hadn't sunk that low.

"And then there's alcohol and hormones. Both can mess up your blood sugar," Dr Flint told him once again. "Not much you can do about your hormones but watch your alcohol intake. Best avoid it altogether."

"OK."

That afternoon, Wayne was discharged from the ward with a tag to wear around his neck, identifying him as a diabetic. He was also given a diabetic's paraphernalia but he had no real will to use it.

Wayne was back in trouble a few days after he left the hospital's sanctuary. While he was sleeping rough, a junkie nicked his equipment. Wayne thought it was funny. He imagined this guy waiting for a high after injecting himself with insulin. Waiting for a very long time.

Then Wayne forgot his appointment with the diabetes specialist nurse. He remembered it only after leaving the skateboard park that night. But what the hell. Making the most of an unfair life seemed much more important than daily injections. With sore eyes and occasional cramps, he trudged along Charles Street, hoping he'd be able to con his way into a gig at The Leadmill. Perhaps he could get a drink there as well. He hoped so because he felt thirsty enough to drink gallons. His tongue was so dry, it kept sticking horribly to the roof of his mouth. He was also feeling tired and nauseous. An ice-cold lager would go down a treat.

Wayne liked to linger in the hospital. He got plenty of care and attention and a couple of the younger nurses were really pretty. On the ward, he was relieved of the responsibility of looking after himself. Someone else made sure he got the right food and drink at the right time, kept his blood sugar in the right ballpark, took care of the organization and routine. When one of the cute nurses looked after him, Wayne mistook the hospital for heaven. For that, it was worth putting up with the doctor's patronizing sermons.

Dr Flint was wearing a wry expression. "Wayne, how many times have they brought you in here in the last few weeks?"

"Dunno."

"Guess."

"Four times?"

"Yes, exactly. Four times. You've learned very quickly how to get yourself admitted but it can't go on, Wayne. We've got to keep you fit and well and out of here. Do you do your injection every day?"

"Yeah."

"Really?"

"Most days."

"Most days isn't enough. It's got to be regular. And you've missed most of your appointments with the specialist nurse."

"Yeah but. . ."

"But what?"

"I dunno. It's hard."

"How about if I arrange a daily visit to her so she can do your injections for you? It's not going to help, is it?"

"I can do injections," Wayne replied.

"You *can*, yes. You can do them very well but you don't. And I suppose you *could* go to the nurse but you'd forget that as well."

Wayne shrugged.

Dr Flint sighed and smiled at the same time. "OK, Wayne. I want you to meet someone who might be able to help. He's an expert and he's so clever, he's a professor. Professor Clayton."

"Yeah?" Wayne said, unenthusiastically. If he was going to be treated like a ten year old, it wasn't worth much of a reply.

"He's got an entirely new way of controlling diabetes."

"I been asking around. What I've heard, you can look after yourself perfect, not miss a dose, not once, and still lose a leg or your sight. So, at the end of the day, why bother?"

"The way Professor Clayton does it, you don't have to bother with injections. He puts something in your body that takes care of the insulin for ever. It's like getting your pancreas working again. That way, you stand a good chance of avoiding the complications – and you don't have to remember to do things."

"Oh?"

"I think you're the ideal candidate for him. Do you want me to fix it for you to see him?"

"Suppose."

Before going to see Wayne, Dr Flint said to Richard Clayton, "I'm failing miserably with this boy, not because of his disease but because I can't get him interested in managing it for himself. If I let him, he'd just hang around the hospital all the time."

"Have you tried him on the pump?"

"He wouldn't be able to afford it. Besides, he'd still be responsible for his own medication. He'd still have to programme the pump, press the right button at the right time to get the right trickle of insulin. You'll see for yourself, he's just not that sort of kid. Responsibility isn't his strong point."

"All right. Let's go and have a chat with him. Sounds like a perfect case."

In a matter of hours, Wayne was installed in the Department of Experimental Medicine, listening to a loud steel band sprinting enthusiastically through Caribbean versions of hit songs for the benefit of the patients. Already Wayne had agreed to try a revolutionary new method of fighting diabetes. The professor bloke was going to inject tiny robots into his bloodstream, as long as his uncle and aunt would sign the consent forms. These robots – nanorobots, he called them – would stay inside him for the rest of his life and they'd swim around monitoring his sugar levels and, when they threatened to rise too much, produce and release insulin. It was great. He was going to be the very first in the world to have them. That meant he'd be important, like the first man on the moon, and he'd be looked after really well by the professor and his nurses. He felt like he was the star of a science fiction film. He'd be walking around with robots on the inside! Terrific.

It was strange to be in a high-dependency ward when he was perfectly well, his episodes under strict control. But he had an excuse to stay put because the professor was doing lots of tests and things on him. In between, Wayne was free to wander around, eager to spot a pretty face. But most of the other patients were ancient and more-or-less bedridden. They came in a variety of flavours: wrinkly, wheezing, blind, bizarrely coloured, gurgling, deathly still, hooked up to a variety of humming, bleeping and flashing machines. Now, Wayne understood why the musicians had played at such volume. They were trying to get their calypso tunes past the greys' exhausted eardrums. Despite the colourful paintings on the walls and occasional musicians strumming in the aisles, the place wasn't exactly a bundle of laughs.

Once he tried one of the side-doors in the ward, curious

about what was behind it. Another wing? A private room? The staff's tea room? But he didn't find out. A nurse came and shooed him away from it. Besides, it had a security lock with a keypad and he didn't know the combination.

The only other young person in the ward was a girl but she was hardly a pretty sight. Maybe she'd been pretty once. It was hard to tell. It looked like she'd had most of her face burned off. Wayne shuddered to think how she must feel about it. At least, like him, she could move around. She wasn't as decrepit as the greys.

One day, Wayne noticed that she had a visitor. It was an Asian girl. When Wayne wandered past, he saw her only from one side but she looked gorgeous. Just what he needed to help him get better. When he spun round and went back towards his own bed, though, Wayne saw the visitor full on. He saw the whole disappointing effect. She wasn't a real looker after all. Like the patient, she had a mutilated face. In a way, the two of them were twins – sisters of disfigurement.

Wayne turned away, not sure if he felt pity or disgust.

6 SKIN

Cassie couldn't remember the last time she'd eaten a meal. It was a complete blank in her mind, unimportant. Since being in hospital, she'd been fed essential nutrients by tube. In a way, she wished that she was still being fed by tube. The act of eating was tediously slow, painful, unpleasant and messy. In her sixteen years, she'd watched her three younger brothers come into the world one-by-one, drool, dribble milk and then eat like chimps at a tea party. Mush in, half of it out again. That was Cassie now. Like baby food, her meal looked as if it had been pre-chewed for convenience. She shovelled it in, swallowed some, ejected some. On top of that, with her one eye, she wasn't good at judging where her mouth was. Some spoonfuls missed the target and ended up coating her etched cheeks. Cassie knew that at mealtimes she put on a distasteful show. And she hated it. Utterly hated it.

The trauma of seeing herself still loomed large, like the unshakeable effect of a grotesque nightmare. Cassie was haunted by that ghoulish face which, she had to keep telling herself, was her own. That's what people would see when they looked at her. That's what they'd see *instead of* her. That's why everyone would struggle to contain their revulsion whenever they met her. The powerful tranquillizers and a counsellor had done their jobs, though, and Cassie was no longer in a complete panic, her stomach churning, her galloping heart at bursting point, her head thudding. She was simply devastated, a long way from coming to terms with this new twist in her already convoluted life. Depressed, she believed she'd been on a downward spiral for far too long.

She felt thoroughly awkward when Taslima was brought to her bedside. The two of them shared a natural kinship which should have provided an instant bond but it didn't. Cassie knew she had to form an opinion about skin grafts based on Taslima's appearance and that made Taslima an exhibit rather than a friend.

Taslima was a living tragedy. She had beautiful long black lustrous hair that contrasted with the scrappy collage of the ravaged right side of her face. It had been painfully reconstructed in nine operations so far. Even so, she had a smile that sometimes outshone the mass of scar tissue.

"What happened?" Cassie asked in a quiet self-conscious voice.

Taslima sat on the bed while Cassie slumped in the easy chair. "I'm a Muslim. I'm supposed to marry my father's choice but. . ." She looked directly at Cassie's face. Forgetting she'd been told that Cassie was from Northern Ireland, Taslima said, "I'm as English as you. I want the same things English girls have. But my family didn't see it like that. They said I brought shame on them – disgraced the family name – by refusing a marriage. My mother threatened to kill herself or send me to Pakistan if I didn't go through with it. And when I didn't, my brothers attacked me with acid, tried to make it so no one would want to marry me ever again. When I left home, my father wouldn't speak to me but he said to the others, 'Losing a daughter isn't important. It's loss of family honour that matters.' I don't suppose he misses me much and, in a way, the acid didn't work. I have a good boyfriend."

Cassie didn't know if her own face could show a blush any more but she felt embarrassed to be drawn so quickly into Taslima's private life. At the mention of a boyfriend, though, Cassie tried to brighten up. "Oh?"

Taslima gave one of her smiles. "If you're going to be disfigured, there's an advantage in making it the face. Friends – boys in particular – can see exactly what they're getting. If they're uncomfortable with it, they wouldn't start anything in the first place. With a face, what you see is what you get. Hidden scars would be much worse. At some point, you'd have to reveal them and wait for a reaction. It must be a terrible moment, waiting for a look of disgust or a shrug of the shoulders, waiting to be rejected or accepted."

Behind her, a boy wandered past. Cassie had seen him before, swaggering through the ward like he owned it. His bearing suggested that he was keen to show he wasn't as ill as everyone else. Yet Cassie knew that appearances can be deceptive. Perhaps he'd be lifeless by morning while all of the others would still be loitering outside death's door, showing no inclination to enter. One thing about the boy was odd, though. In this ward, he was a misfit because he was young. Cassie nodded vaguely in his direction but he didn't notice because he was eyeing Taslima.

"You've never taken to wearing one of those things?" Cassie put her blotchy hands, no longer in bags, in front of her face.

Taslima was concentrating on Cassie's mangled words but this time she failed to understand them. "Pardon?"

"Do you wear a veil thing?"

"A burkha?"

"Yes, that's it."

"A burkha's a sack. Why should I wear a sack? I don't have a problem with letting people see how I look. I'm different, that's all."

Taslima was wearing a flowing chiffon dress in bright yellow. A delicate narrow piece of the fabric lay across her neck and fell over her shoulders. To Cassie, it looked elegant and sexy but she wondered if the outfit was hiding anything unsightly about Taslima's throat and shoulders.

"Does it hurt?" Cassie asked.

Taslima was still thinking about other people's reaction to her appearance. "It hurts a lot when people stare, it hurts a bit when they turn away, but it doesn't hurt at all when little kids say, 'Mummy what's wrong with that girl's face?' You have to get used to it. Children are so natural and curious, aren't they?" Then she added, "Physically, it doesn't hurt. Not now."

"How did your friends react?" Cassie said.

"I didn't have many when it happened. Plenty of relatives, not many friends. I've got more friends now. New ones."

Cassie did not dare to ask if they'd befriended her out of pity or because they liked her. "Did Dr Staunton tell you what happened to me?"

Taslima nodded. "I know about religious hatred." She paused before adding, "But acid can't tell the difference.

Muslim skin, Catholic skin, Protestant skin. It's all the same."

Cassie and Taslima had so much in common. They both had their funny faces, their splintered families, and a brush with fundamentalists. Cassie could have been targeted specifically in Belfast because of her family or the acid might have been intended for any passing Catholic. Cassie didn't know for sure but she feared the worst. She could have asked Taslima dozens more questions but two were particularly important to her. She looked straight at her visitor and said, "Are you happy with your face?"

"I'm happier in myself. I wish it hadn't happened – I'd be a fool not to – but, if it hadn't, I wouldn't have met my boyfriend, I wouldn't have the friends I've got now. No. I'm sorry about getting hurt but I can't live with a grudge against my family all my life. I don't believe in regretting."

"Would you have a new face if you were offered one?"

Taslima hesitated for several seconds. "I don't know. I don't think so. I'd be too scared. Besides, it took me ages – I went through a lot of pain – to get this one and I'm used to it now. I invested so much in it and a lot of people worked so hard to give me it so, no, I couldn't get rid of it now. It's *me*. It's who I am, take it or leave it."

Cassie nodded but she knew she wasn't as brave as Taslima. She had never considered herself to be vain or fussy but she wanted to look good. She didn't have to have a face like a film star, she just didn't want to be ugly. Clearly, Taslima was beautiful on the inside, but on the outside. . . Cassie's injuries were even more extensive so, if she followed in Taslima's footsteps, she'd be even more unsightly. She wasn't convinced that she could ever be content to live a life like that. She didn't want to listen to everyone telling her that she could still have a full and rewarding life. That would only remind her that it was going to be hell. No, she *really wanted* a full and rewarding life.

The thought of a new face was enormously scary but, compared to Taslima's skin grafts, a transplant was the easy option.

Dr Staunton tried hard to contain a self-satisfied smile. "Are you sure, Cassie?"

"Certain."

"I'm pleased. This way, you'll get your good looks back."

"*My* good looks?"

"Well, not yours exactly but not the donor's either. Remember, to a large extent what anyone looks like is down to bone structure. Someone else's face won't alter your bone structure. After the operation, you'll look partly like yourself and partly like the donor."

"The donor."

"Yes," Dr Staunton said, "we've got to look into that. There's a couple of possibilities I've got to check out. I'll get photos for you if there's a suitable match."

Cassie could hardly bare to think about it, yet Dr Staunton was acting like a fashion designer who was about to change Cassie's image and was offering to show her pictures of supermodel outfits. She was too choked to respond.

"I've spoken to your dad about a transplant and he agreed to it as long as you want us to go ahead. He said I should point out that changing your appearance is no bad thing in your situation. The police think it's a help as well."

Cassie let out a derisory grunt. They'd already provided her with a new identity. For even greater security, they were now keen to see her with a new face. "If – when – I look different, the bad guys – as Dad calls them – won't recognize me, but what about friends? What'll they think?"

"Your friends?" Dr Staunton sat down. "When we first bump into someone new we judge them by their appearance, it's true. Maybe we shouldn't but we do. It's human nature. It's not like that with friends, though. Your face will have altered but they'll already know what you're really like so they won't be judging you. They don't reassess their friendship every time you change your hairstyle, do they? Appearance won't matter to them."

Distracted, Cassie turned her tender neck to fix her eye on the eight men who were gathering between the rows of beds.

"Ah," Dr Staunton said with a smile. "The old folk like this. It's the Bolsterstone Male Voice Choir. We give them a bit of space in the department and a captive audience. It's practice for them, therapy for us. Music lowers blood pressure, raises spirits, shortens recovery time. That's what the research says anyway."

Cassie repositioned her head to look again at the surgeon. "When will you. . .?"

"First things first, Cassie. Let's see about a donor. One might crop up today or it might take a month. Or more."

Cassie turned away, too nervous and upset to talk.

*

OK, her eyesight wasn't up to scratch, but Cassie thought she saw. . . Well, what she definitely saw was Dr Staunton guiding a middle-aged woman into one of the side rooms. Dr Staunton was treating her with a great deal of respect, like some civic dignitary ushering the Queen around a new building without actually touching her. The surgeon's hand was near the small of her visitor's back but not in contact. At the door, Dr Staunton punched a number into the lock, opened the door and stepped aside, letting her guest float inside. Before she went in, Dr Staunton looked around as if she were checking that no one was watching, as if she were ashamed.

In fact, Dr Staunton did have an audience. Two nurses were trying to pretend that they were unconcerned when they could hardly contain their curiosity about the visitor. That boy was standing around as well. He didn't seem to be interested in the woman. Instead, he was concentrating on the code that Dr Staunton used to get into the room. By the disgruntled look on his face, he hadn't caught whatever he wanted to see.

He was a strange boy, thin enough to be gravely ill but it was probably his natural physique. A gale could easily have blown him away, unless he was standing side-on to the wind. He was slightly taller than Cassie and rather scruffy. When he had his own clothes on, he was very scruffy. His jet black hair had been unkempt and too long but the hairdresser who serviced the ward had recently sorted him out. Now, he seemed made up about his appearance and he strutted around even more than before. He was the only one in the ward who seemed happy to be in hospital. Cassie knew that she shouldn't assess anyone by their appearance – especially not now – but she couldn't help thinking that he didn't look like the intelligent sort. Yet, for all his quirks, he was bizarrely attractive. His carefree face had instant and innocent charm. He also had an appealingly mischievous grin. Cassie shook her head. She was thinking that way about him, she told herself, only because she'd been starved of boys, because there was no competition.

Now, though, they shared more than a wing of the hospital. They glanced at each other and realized that they were both nosy about the goings-on in the ward.

Wayne took a few steps towards her, stopped and said, "I've noticed you."

"Oh? Why?"

"Because. . ." He hesitated. "Because you're not grey."

"You really mean, because of my face."

"Suppose," he muttered. "You can't miss it, like."

That was it. Cassie shrank back into her own shell. She guessed that he meant no harm. He was just stating an undeniable fact. And after all, she'd prompted his display of straight-talking. But she hadn't yet had a chance to get accustomed to blunt honesty. Perhaps she wouldn't have to – if she had her transplant soon. Then, she'd have to get accustomed to wearing a dead girl's face instead.

RADICALS 7

Wayne had to admit that his first attempt to talk to the girl down the ward wasn't an overwhelming success. He didn't know why. She'd just taken bad at something he'd said. He wasn't going to let it bother him – not much ever did – because, well, she wasn't anyone's idea of a decent catch. She was a stunner all right but not the sort of stunner he had in mind. She had only two things going for her: she was young and she was there. Maybe three things. He'd never seen a girl in her nightclothes before and she looked all right from the neck down. If she wasn't disfigured under her nightie, she'd be really tasty.

Deciding to try again, next time he wandered into her part of the ward he caught her eye and nodded. In response, her face formed a smile of a sort. He thought it was a smile anyway. At least she didn't recoil from him so he took it as a good sign. Awkwardly, he went over to her bedside and said, "Is that some sort of accent you've got?"

"Can't you tell?"

"Not really."

Cassie knew her mouth warped her words and disguised her voice. She couldn't blame the boy for that. "I'm from Northern Ireland."

"What's your name?"

"Cassie." Cassie O'Rourke wasn't her real name but only

her father and a few top people in the security force knew that. "And you?"

"Wayne. Wayne Wingate."

"That's a mouthful." For Cassie, everything was a mouthful.

"It's worse."

"Oh?"

"I never knew my mum. She abandoned me. But she was an Internet freak. A right addict."

"So?"

"I came along at the same time as the world-wide web. Second best to the www, me. Only thing I got out of it were a name."

It dawned on Cassie. "Not Wayne W Wingate?"

"William."

"Oh dear."

"Don't you hate parents who think they're funny?" Wayne said, putting his endearing grin on show.

Cassie shrugged. "I wouldn't know about that." Changing the subject quickly, she asked, "Why are you here? You look fit."

"Everyone says that."

"So?"

He pulled the tag out from under his shirt. "I got diabetes."

"You can't have sweets, then."

Wayne thought about it for a moment. "Life ain't sweet."

"There's worse things than missing out on chocolate."

Unable to make out her words, he asked, "What's that?"

"Never mind."

"They're fixing me with robots."

"Robots?"

As best he could, Wayne told her about Richard Clayton's nanomedicine. "I'm the world number one, me. What about you? You got to look on the bright side. At least everyone don't ask why you're here."

"No."

"How are they fixing you up?"

"I'm going to have a transplant."

"What? You're gonna get someone else's *face*?"

Cassie took a breath through her misshapen mouth. Immediately going on the defensive, she said, "I know you're going to say it's horrid and wrong but you're not stuck with. . ."

Wayne looked hurt. "I weren't going to say that. I think a face transplant's great." Struck by a bright idea, he said, "You could go through a thingy – a catalogue – and pick a good 'un, a real winner."

Thrown by Wayne's reaction, Cassie replied, "She'd have to be dead."

"Pity." Wayne hesitated and then added, "Till you get your new face, you could wear a balaclava."

Cassie was horrified. Was that his idea of a joke? Was it a serious suggestion that was supposed to be helpful? But Cassie was horrified for another reason. Her mind turned to the terrorists back home. She always imagined that the ones who killed her mum and little brothers wore balaclavas. In her mind's eye, she saw them creeping up to the back of the house on that dark and chilly winter's afternoon, throwing the bomb through the window. Everything in the living room, including her mum and the boys, had been punctured with the nails that they'd packed around the explosive. Cassie wasn't the first in her family to be mutilated.

Wayne was still talking. "When it got cold, I wore this balaclava. It were right good because it scared old women." He looked at Cassie and stopped. "You OK?"

"No." She rolled on to her side and pulled the blanket over her disfigurement.

It had been going so well, Wayne thought, till Cassie took it into her head to turn funny. Wayne wondered what the girl's problem was – apart from the obvious. He stood there for a few seconds before shrugging and going back to his own bed without an answer.

On the way, he heard a commotion behind him. He spun round to see that a man had burst into the ward at a run. He was heading towards Cassie's bed. He didn't make it, though, because a bouncer hurtled up behind him and brought him down in a magnificently executed rugby tackle. In seconds, the intruder was handcuffed and led away, shouting something about his wife.

Unaware of the excitement, Cassie remained under her sheets.

An hour later, when Wayne asked what all the fuss had been about, Professor Clayton told him that it had all been a misunderstanding. The man had just received some devastating news about his wife and he'd dashed into the wrong ward. That was it. All perfectly innocent. Security had taken care of it. Nothing to be concerned about. Disappointed, Wayne lost interest almost straightaway but he did wonder why some sort of fed was stationed outside the Department of Experimental Medicine. He hoped that the police weren't keeping him under surveillance. He didn't relish being arrested again as soon as he was discharged.

When Professor Clayton and Dr Staunton went into one of the secret rooms, Wayne kept an eye on them and he caught sight of the last digit of the entry code: 7. All he needed was the second number and he had the complete sequence. He didn't know why he was so keen to crack the combination but it gave him something to do while he waited for the big injection. There was no going back after that. He'd be ruled by robots for ever. He'd be kept under intense observation for three weeks then, if all was well, he'd be off, no more a diabetic. He had to agree to come back once a week for check-ups. Professor Clayton also said that, to repay the department for his revolutionary treatment, he would be called in now and again to meet other patients. It was a small price, he'd argued, for a normal life.

In one of the private rooms that Hilary used to talk to her celebrity sponsors with the confidentiality that they demanded, she waited for Richard to tell her why he'd asked to have a quiet word with her.

"You know I'm anxious that the department uses its expertise well – for the good of medicine and ordinary mortals," Richard began.

"Yes?" Hilary sat on the unoccupied bed and leaned back on her straightened arms while Richard prowled around restlessly.

"Well, I can only do that if my research funds keep rolling in."

"And they're not?" Hilary guessed.

"Right now, I'm scraping the bottom of the barrel." Richard sighed. "We both know your work and mine are easily the most promising in the department. Controversial – we don't always see eye to eye – but we're way out in front, yes?"

"What's your point, Richard?"

"You know I've got nanorobots that'll adjust sugar levels by making and releasing insulin. You know I've developed ones that'll deliver drugs to the site of a disease or scrub the deposits from arteries. But I've kept quiet about some that'll sense abnormal tissue growth and other signs of ageing, nipping it in the bud. . ."

Hilary interrupted him with ironic laughter. "So that's what this chat's all about!"

"What?"

"You criticize me for being that close," she said, bringing her thumb and finger together, "to cosmetic surgery and you're at it yourself!"

It was Richard's turn to interrupt. "Not surgery, no. It's just that I can use nanotechnology to preserve the elasticity of skin – that's wrinkles taken care of – and keep the hair in good condition for life. It's relatively easy to make robots that can snap up free radicals before they wreak havoc."

Hilary was still shaking her head wryly. "Not surgery, no, but anti-ageing isn't for the good of medicine and ordinary mortals. It's pampering to the vanity of the rich – just like I

44

do, according to you." She paused and then said, "How have you tested these cosmetic robots?"

"Laboratory mice and chimpanzees."

"No human subjects yet?"

"No."

"So you want my contacts! You want names of people who're so desperate they'll throw money at you if there's a chance you can keep them fit and looking young."

"That's a little crude but. . ."

"Don't get me wrong, Richard," Hilary said with a grin. "I'm all for your conversion to my way of thinking. Principles are all very well. They give you something to cling to as you go under. You've decided not to go under but to grab opportunities instead. Your cash crisis will have done you a favour if it's made you less smug and more practical. I think you're right to fund your more important work by exploiting the vanity of the ageing rich. Where's the harm in that? Yes, I could be persuaded to give you a few names. . ."

"What's the deal?"

"Come on! I expect support. I don't expect criticism in departmental meetings. I expect someone to put my name forward to the Human Resources Committee."

"It's bothered you, that, hasn't it? You like the sound of Professor Staunton."

Hilary didn't have to respond. "I know a man, a bit withered, bald, did some big films in the seventies. Name of Arthur. He'd like to look like he did back then – a dashing screen idol. He's just been asked to play a pensioner in a TV soap and that was the last straw. Forget growing old gracefully, he wants firm-fleshed youth. He's loaded and he's coming in the day after tomorrow."

"Thanks, Hilary."

"I know plenty of others trying to cheat ageing, plenty in the music business trying to conform to today's idea of beauty. I could supply more contacts if things go well."

"OK."

Hilary nodded. "You see, nobody's satisfied with their appearance, particularly not women. Even people who look perfect to the rest of us see flaws in themselves and want them put right. They think they can be better than perfect."

It was clear from Richard's face that he disapproved. "Sad. Most people's problems aren't skin deep, even when they think they are. *Especially* when they think they are. A new face or body image doesn't cure disillusionment or insecurity. Self-esteem doesn't come in a bottle: it can't be injected or transplanted."

"No," Hilary agreed, "but you've realized there's something to be gained from giving them what they want. Besides, they pay enormous sums to shrinks on top of their cosmetic surgery. You stick to signs of ageing and let their psychoanalysts fleece them to straighten out their brains." She stood up. "I'll tell you what, though. People like Arthur don't want to be guinea pigs. They'll give you money to develop the procedure but they'll want to see results on lesser mortals before they go for it themselves."

Regretting that a shortage of funds was forcing his hand, Richard announced, "I'm going to see Wayne Wingate."

"Big day today, is it?"

"Yeah."

Just before her colleague opened the door, a thought occurred to Hilary. Richard was an intelligent man. He'd know that he'd need to test his treatment before he enticed any superstar clients so he must already have a plan. "Am I right in thinking you're going to do more than cure Wingate's diabetes?"

Richard hesitated. "He's lucky. I'm doing him a favour by giving him protection against cancer, heart disease and ageing."

Hilary shook her head at his double standards. "What happened to your theory about going to great lengths to stay on the right side of ethics? Is that just something you say in public?"

Richard looked uncomfortable for a moment. "If I'm going to improve everyone's lot, I've realized I've got to be flexible."

Hilary asked, "What happens if it all goes wrong, Richard? Once your robots have descaled arteries, where will they end up and what will they do? What if the robots decide a heart is a cancerous growth?"

Richard was quieter than Hilary but he had the same absolute confidence in his medical methods. "They won't. To quote you," he said firmly, "it works." With that, he strode back out on to the ward.

8 FOOD

The doctors in the Department of Experimental Medicine were regarded by the patients as endlessly caring yet deeply sinister at the same time. It was because they always seemed to know more than they were prepared to discuss. It was because they had power over health and disease, over life and death.

Richard Clayton handed the sealed polythene bag to Wayne and said, "Here it is."

Wayne toyed with the fluid-filled bag for a moment. Unimpressed, he replied, "Looks like water."

Professor Clayton smiled. "Expensive water. There's years of research in there. The nanorobots are invisible to the naked eye, of course."

Wayne returned the sachet. "You sure they're in there?"

"I need you to lie on the bed for the next hour while this drips directly into your bloodstream."

Wayne shrugged.

"You understand it's a one-way trip?"

"You've said often enough."

"They'll start straightaway and stay inside you permanently. If, in the future, any stop working or you lose a lot through injury and bleeding, the others will detect it and replicate themselves till you're back up to strength."

Wayne nodded.

"They don't have batteries or anything like that so they don't run down. They're powered just like you are – with food. It's your body's processing of food that fuels your muscles and now the same chemicals will fuel your nanorobots as well. They tap in to your metabolism. As long as you eat, your nanorobots'll never be exhausted."

"OK," said Wayne.

"If you understand all that, are you ready?"

"Yeah."

A nurse was standing there, expecting to insert the needle in Wayne's arm, hook up the bag above his bed and connect the two but Professor Clayton wouldn't let go of the reins. He was like a boy determined not to surrender the console of a favourite game. He was going to carry out the procedure himself, to make absolutely sure. The nurse was reduced to spectator.

Once he was satisfied that the drip was in place and working, Professor Clayton straightened up and pronounced, "Right, you're on the way. The first person anywhere to have your diabetes controlled completely automatically with internal robots. No more insulin injections, no more episodes, no reason to have Diet Coke rather than the real thing. There'll be all sorts of benefits. You're still dependent on insulin, of course, because we all are. Without it, we starve to death. The difference is, diabetics inject it, my pancreas makes it for me, and your robots make it for you. That means, with a bit of luck, you'll avoid any of the long-term complications of diabetes."

Wayne looked down at his bared, punctured arm where

invisible ranks of robots – the sugar police – were marching into his bloodstream. "I don't feel any different."

"You won't feel anything at all. I'm not aware of my pancreas and pretty soon you'll forget your nanorobots are there."

But unbeknown to Wayne, several types of robot had begun to motor around his body.

For the next forty-eight hours, Wayne was watched, monitored and pampered as if he were royalty. His blood and urine were treated like gold. He could hardly go anywhere without a nurse or Professor Clayton saying, "Time for your next blood test."

"Again? All right. I'll do it."

If they let him analyse his own blood, a nurse watched him like a hawk. The staff couldn't afford any mistakes. Every point on the graph of his blood glucose level had to be spot on. The slightest sign of a trend brought Richard Clayton rushing out to examine him. But all was fine. The time for his insulin injections came and went and his blood sugar hardly wavered. It stayed resolutely in the safe zone. The diabetic paraphernalia stayed in its box. Results coming back from the lab were reassuringly blank: Wayne's urine remained free of glucose and ketone bodies. He showed no sign of fatigue or extraordinary thirst or fainting or sickness or blurred vision and his glucose did not drop to a level that threatened a hypo. No highs, no lows, no blackouts, nothing. Just a normal day. The sugar police were on patrol and in control.

When the nurses weren't demanding samples, they were measuring his blood pressure, checking that his eyesight remained clear, and putting him through fitness tests. He was also sent for a whole-body scan so that Professor Clayton could assess his overall health and, in the future, monitor any changes. "I expect healthy blood vessels particularly in your eyes and kidneys. And I want to see a healthy heart and nice open arteries everywhere."

Wayne also felt perky because he filled in the last gap in the security code for the side-rooms. The full number was 1987 – the year that the department was founded. He caught sight of it when Professor Clayton invited him into one of the rooms, punched in the combination and held the door open for him.

Inside, it was just another hospital room but plush and private and beautifully decorated. There was the usual hi-tech bed but there was also a bathroom, a shower, a television with DVD player, a hi-fi system, a window overlooking a garden, a huge array of gadgets and, in one of several easy chairs, an old man.

Professor Clayton said, "I've told this gentleman – Arthur – a bit about you and your treatment. He's interested. Can you tell him how you feel?"

Wayne shrugged. "OK."

"Go on, then," the man in the chair said impatiently.

"No, I mean, I'm OK, like."

"Just OK, Wayne?" Professor Clayton prompted. "Is that all?"

"I'm good."

Arthur smiled. It wasn't so much a sign of friendship but an indication that he believed he'd only get what he wanted from Wayne by appearing to be friendly. "Have you had any after-effects from your treatment?" His deep voice seemed to fill the room.

"No. I'm fine."

The man was wearing designer clothes that probably cost a fortune. He was almost certainly older than he looked. Wayne suspected that he was wearing make-up to hide the lines in his face and his full head of dark hair had undoubtedly been bought rather than grown. He said, "Do you feel sick at all?"

Wayne shook his head. "I feel good. Better than I've been for ages."

"Thirsty?" asked Professor Clayton.

"Not really. My eyes aren't sore and I'm not knackered for a change. No cramps either. It's right good."

"Any pain, dizziness or tingling sensations?"

Wayne shook his head. "Nothing."

"Are they looking after you well?" Arthur said.

"It's great here. Can't move without tripping over nurses. Nice ones at that. Live music, as well." He pulled a face to show it wasn't to his taste.

Arthur glanced significantly at Professor Clayton and nodded slightly.

Professor Clayton said, "It's far too early to be totally sure, of course, but all the signs are excellent. Wayne's level of fitness is soaring. The nanorobots are performing well up to expectation, if not better. So that's all for now, thanks, Wayne. I'll let you out and you can go back. I'm sure a nurse will want you for another test."

The second person who wanted him was a wound-up Cassie. She waited for the nurse to leave with the latest reading of Wayne's blood pressure and then asked, "Did you ever see *The Tree House*?"

Wayne frowned. "Which tree house?"

"No. The *Tree House*. The film."

"Doubt it."

Trying to stir a memory, Cassie said, "An old one."

"What was it about?"

An attempt at a pout died on Cassie's lips. "A tree house," she answered. "At least, a man who lived in one."

"No."

"When you went in there," she pointed at the private room where Professor Clayton had taken Wayne, "did you see the man they took in?"

"Did I see what?"

"A man."

"Yeah," answered Wayne, wondering what the fuss was all about. "Arthur or something."

"Well, he was the spitting image of the man who lived in the tree house – the main actor, with a few years added on."

Wayne pushed out his bottom lip and shrugged.

"And the other day, I'm sure I saw Dr Staunton with a woman who was just like Claire What's-her-name who used to do a stupid game show on the box."

"Used to do a what?"

"A TV game show."

Wayne thought about it, the cogs of his brain stirring slowly, and then said with a grin, "You're seeing stars."

"You don't believe me."

"I do," he replied. "I just don't know if your eyesight's up to the job."

Cassie let out a long breath angrily but she didn't walk away. She'd used her curiosity about the visitors to the department only as an excuse to open a conversation with the one person of her own age in the ward. She hadn't yet started to say what she really wanted to talk about.

"Any news?" Wayne nodded towards her face.

It was the cue she needed but, suddenly feeling vulnerable, Cassie sat down on Wayne's bed. With relief and dread, she took two photographs of girls out of her pocket and showed him the first.

Wayne was impressed. "Mmm. Nice. Very nice. Who is she?"

With a tear in her eye, Cassie answered, "Me."

"You? But it doesn't look. . . I didn't recognize you."

"I've got to keep a photo of the real me."

She gave him the second snapshot. It was an older girl, perhaps eighteen. Very short blonde hair, very large earrings.

Wayne soon came to a verdict. "Quite nice," he said, "but not as nice as . . . well, you – before."

"I've got to keep a reminder of me because *that's* what I'll look like soon."

"Hey! This is your new face," Wayne exclaimed happily, examining the second photo again.

Her emotions in turmoil, Cassie collapsed on to his bed and burst into tears.

"But you should be pleased," Wayne said towards her heaving shoulders. "You're going to look . . . OK." He didn't know what to do. He reached out to touch her back but withdrew his hand before he made contact. Having run out of words, he just stood there helplessly while a nurse dashed over, escorted Cassie back to her bed, and called for the counsellor.

Now that Wayne had got used to Cassie's appearance, he thought she was all right – even if she did crack up at regular intervals for no obvious reason. He realized that he felt neither pity nor disgust for her after all. The way he saw it now, she did not deserve either. She was just a person who looked different. Lots of people looked a bit weird, a bit different. And anyway, the hospital was going to fix her up pretty good. He'd accept her how she was now or how she'd become. It wasn't as if he was thinking of her as a girlfriend so it didn't bother him. But he thought she'd be happier in herself if she turned heads for the right reason. Perhaps then she wouldn't crack up so much.

9 ANTIBODIES

Cassie was sitting rigidly in her chair, virtually petrified, holding a mirror between herself and that ghoulish face. In the glass, Cassie was following Dr Staunton's soft finger as it slowly traced an oval outline where the scalpel would be inserted and the flesh levered up. Horrified, Cassie was reminded of the dotted line on a cut-out coupon.

"I'll take the donor's face, with its muscles, nerves and blood vessels, and attach it to your underlying bone. You'll hardly see the join. It'll be sewn under the chin here and there may be a slight scar but it'll be out of sight." The finger came round Cassie's jawbone and upwards. "Your ears are fine – luckily – so the transplant will come in front of them. We're then into your scalp above the hair line. You'll be shaved, of course, but when your hair regrows – which won't take long – it'll hide any fine scarring. I wouldn't expect to leave any, though. It'll be *your* hair, by the way, grown according to your own body's recipe through the donor's transplanted follicles." The forefinger reached the apex and then began the return journey. "It'll be exactly the same on this side with the new face coming right up close to your ear, behind the jaw and under the chin. That's it. X-rays tell me your bone's unscathed so I won't have to manipulate it. That means you won't look completely different because you'll keep your own bone structure. I'll remodel the missing part of your nose with cartilage so it's just like it used to be. Yes? You don't want me to reshape it while I'm at it?"

Cassie was in shock. She couldn't think straight so she forgot that she'd always believed her nose was too big. She just shook her head.

"Fine. While you're under general anaesthetic, I'll take the opportunity to insert a prosthetic eye – so realistic no one will realize it's artificial – and add some tissue to your gums and tongue on one side. That'll help your speech, teeth and eating. And I'll finish off the skin grafts on your hands. All right, Cassie?" Hilary knew that Cassie had lost the ability to turn as white as a sheet so she had to ask in case nausea was getting the better of her.

"I think so, but it's. . ."

"I know. It's making you woozy but I've got to give you the complete picture, I'm afraid. That's the policy. So you know exactly what you're agreeing to. I don't have a choice. Now don't panic about this next bit because it's all under control." Dr Staunton took the mirror from her patient's hand and said, "You might have heard of rejection. People having transplants sometimes reject the foreign tissue. Their immune system opens hostilities against the transplant and makes antibodies to kill it. This won't happen with you because you'll take pills to stop it. This is important, Cassie. Very important. It's called an immunosuppressant drug and it'll make sure your body doesn't reject your new face. I'll knock out your immune system with the drug just before the operation. Then the transplant should bed in nicely. After, you'll take the pills for ever, I think. Because you're the first,

I'm not entirely sure, though. I'm not making any promises but it might well be that we can ease back on the tablets at some point in the future and see if your immune system's got used to the face and isn't making antibodies to destroy it any more. If that happens, you might not need to take any more drugs. I really don't know. Still, remembering to take pills isn't a big deal and there're no significant side-effects. Just a bit of diarrhoea and, with an immune system below-par, you'll pick up colds and that sort of thing a bit more easily."

Cassie swallowed. "What'd be the first signs of rejection?"

Dr Staunton grimaced. "We don't have to dwell on this, Cassie. You've heard of gangrene and people with frost bite losing a toe or whatever. The first signs of rejection would be a bit like the start of gangrene. There'd be plenty of time to spot it and top up the pills again. The danger comes days after the first signs. That's when an immune system without the drug would rally enough antibodies to launch a full-scale attack on the transplant. You'll have the drug so there's no need to worry about it."

"But what if the drug didn't work and I rejected the face? You're saying it'd turn red and black – something like that – and drop off? That'd be. . ." She shuddered.

The surgeon interrupted. "I'm saying you don't have to worry about it, Cassie. You just take the tablets every day, without fail, and everything'll be fine. It's called tolerance therapy and it's a very powerful anti-rejection drug. It works."

Cassie winced, trying to control her emotions. She had to get off the terrible topic of rejection before she gagged.

"What about . . . you know . . . smiling, frowning and all that?"

Dr Staunton nodded. "A new face is useless unless the nerves in charge of movement and feeling are regenerated. That's the facial nerve and the three branches of the trigeminal nerve. It's not that complicated. And the muscles of course. I'm transferring the donor's muscles and they'll survive long enough for the reconnected nerves and blood vessels to heal and grow, providing you with feeling, movement and expression. I've checked the regeneration speed of your nerve tissue and it's fantastic. Even so, the muscles will be sluggish at first. You'll need a few lessons, a bit of physiotherapy, but you'll get complete control. You'll be able to look surprised, delighted, whatever. But watch out," she added in a low playful voice, "because you'll be able to look embarrassed again as well."

Cassie tried to smile but failed. "What happened to the donor?"

"Don't worry. We've checked absolutely everything. She was completely free of disease. You can't pick anything up from her tissue. She died in a car crash. She sustained a lot of injuries but only a couple of bruises to her face."

To Cassie, it sounded as if Dr Staunton was pleased that the young woman had had the decency to die in a way that hadn't damaged her face. Even if medicine regarded her death as a lucky event and her body as a resource, Cassie couldn't. She felt uneasy about benefiting from the death of another human being. "What about her family?"

"All of her immediate family were in the car with her. An

uncle was willing to donate her body to science if it would help someone else have a better life."

Cassie didn't ask if he'd been paid off, in case she didn't like the answer.

"So . . . what do you think, Cassie?"

"It's not easy." But as soon as the final word fell out of her ridiculous mouth as *eashy*, Cassie knew that she'd go ahead.

"No pressure, but everything's in place. A suitable donor, your dad's authorization, an operating theatre, a supply of the drug, the greatest transplant surgeon in the world. All I need is your say-so."

"When would you do it?"

Dr Staunton replied, "Oh, I always think, once you've made your mind up, it's best to get things like this over with straightaway, don't you?"

"Straightaway?"

Dr Staunton nodded.

Cassie's remaining eyelid closed half-heartedly in a parody of prayer.

Scrubbed spotless and swathed in a sterile gown, Hilary stood between the two beds, between the two motionless girls. Both looked as if they had receding hairlines because they'd been shaved from their ears to a point high on their foreheads. From two damaged human beings, one unconscious and the other dead, Hilary was going to fashion one perfect living model. For Hilary, it was a creative process. The operation she was about to perform was a scientist's work of art. And she was surrounded by the tools of her trade: from old-fashioned scalpels to surgical microlasers and three-dimensional virtual reality views of her patient's head. She had an anaesthetist standing by and five assistants. They all knew their roles, they all knew that today they were making history. It was likely that the complete procedure would extend through the afternoon, evening and into tomorrow morning but they were prepared for a long haul. If any of them lost concentration, got tired or felt ill, Hilary had substitutes standing by. Hilary herself was the only one who could not be replaced but she was on a high, unlikely to notice the passing of time. Anyway, she had thought of everything. She had a stimulant standing by as well. If she started to flag, one of the nurses was responsible for injecting her.

She looked at Cassie's torn and tortured face and then at the matched donor. All of her research, all of her determination, all of those punches below the belt, were worth it for this moment in time. In her eyes, she had neither bribed nor bullied the donor's uncle. The money was incidental. She had simply refused to budge until she'd persuaded him that no one gained from cremating his niece. It was such a waste to reduce God's work, nature's work, to ashes when it could heal a fellow human being, an utterly desperate young girl. That was the way, Hilary had argued sincerely and skilfully, to give meaning to a tragically short life. The death would be pointless otherwise. She promised him that the recipient would not end up looking the same as his brother's girl. Hilary also asked him to think what his niece would have wanted. Surely the fact that she carried a donor card meant she would have wanted her body to benefit someone else. Besides, Hilary assured him that she would arrange a cremation of her remains straightaway afterwards. No one else would even have to know that her body was incomplete, if that would help him deal with his sad loss.

In the operating theatre, Hilary and the team were savouring a few seconds of quiet contemplation before they embarked on hours of intense, painstaking and intricate work. In that moment, the isolated room felt like a becalmed ship and the whole world seemed to be holding its breath. Breaking the spell from behind her mask, Hilary said, "OK, everyone. The patient's immune system is completely down so we're going to keep this infection-free. No one takes any risks at all." For Cassie's safety, each member of the medical team had been thoroughly vetted and declared free of any sort of bug. "I don't need to remind you that we don't get a second shot at this. We get it right first time or we ruin a girl's life." She nodded towards the window and someone behind it turned on the CD player that would provide soft chill-out music to keep them cool and composed throughout the lengthy ordeal. "Let's get going."

She turned to the inert Cassie. To sculpt a new face, first the damaged one had to be carefully detached. The artist in Hilary needed a blank canvas. Later, she'd use the laser to cut to a precise depth but, to start, there was nothing like the human touch, nothing like a deftly handled scalpel. "Swab," Hilary demanded.

WOOL 10

Cassie felt as if she had slithered down a snake to start again back at square one. Her head throbbed. Her face shrieked with pain. She was aware of a tube attached to her arm, a catheter, and dressings pulling at the skin around her neck and ears when she swallowed. She tried to open her eye but the eyelid would not budge. She could open her mouth but she couldn't form a recognizable word. At once, Cassie refused to play the game of real life. It had become too much, too rough. There were far more snakes than ladders.

She slipped back into semi-consciousness, into a world where she had a mother and a father and three brothers. Cassie knew it was just a muddled dream but the effects of the anaesthetic made it seem so believable. She was back in Belfast, in the living room with her mum and the boys, but they couldn't see or hear her. She was shouting at them, waving her arms madly, and they were simply ignoring her as if she were the ghost.

Outside, it was pouring. Each leaf on the tree convulsed every time a drop struck it so the entire foliage seemed to be quaking. And at the window, a miserable sodden Bernie was clawing at the glass, desperate to get in. Liquid was dripping from her hair, nose and chin and rolling down her cheeks. Behind her, though, a wide-shouldered man in a balaclava was strolling unhurriedly towards her as if he'd got all the time in the world to execute his plan. Through the terrifying holes in the wool, Cassie could see that his eyes were hard yet his red lips were curved into a smile as he closed in on Bernie and the house.

Cassie knew this was not right. She knew this was not how it had happened. Bernie hadn't been around when her mum and brothers were attacked. Her mum and brothers weren't around when Bernie was saturated with petrol and burned. The hallucination was a montage of important moments in her life but the same man in a balaclava straddled both tragedies, drawing them together in her mind.

Cassie tore herself away from the image of Bernie and yelled another warning at her family but still they paid her no attention. They didn't seem to want to know that there'd be an explosion, that nails would fly like darts across the room. In the jumbled delusion, Cassie noticed for the first time that her mum was holding a short thin knife, possibly a scalpel. There was a bright flash of yellow and Cassie's silent voice screamed.

"You're nearly back with us. Good. I'm just taking a look in your eye, Cassie. Sorry, it'll be bright."

Cassie just wanted to lie there. She didn't want to have to figure out who was speaking, what was happening, and why someone was pulling at the skin around her eye. She longed to sleep and wake up years younger with her old identity, her true name and a normal family life. She'd had enough of both horrifying hallucinations and reality.

"I'm just going to change a dressing, Cassie. You might feel a slight tug. It's nothing to worry about."

"Watch out!" Cassie uttered. Her speech sounded like a baby's, mispronounced and scarcely comprehensible.

"Sorry. I'm being as gentle as possible."

"He's coming for Bernie or Mum. I don't know."

Dr Staunton couldn't make out what her patient was trying to say but she recognized distress. "Nurse! Diazepam, please."

The girl in the silky yellow dress had a boyfriend all right. He was hugging her fervently as if his life depended on it. Cassie watched her faraway, almost ecstatic expression for a while, then walked slowly around the couple like a camera operator capturing the scene for a romantic film. Leaving behind the girl's profile, her boyfriend came gradually into Cassie's view. With increasing alarm, Cassie realized who he was. Or at least she recognized what type of man he was. His head was enveloped in wool and his outsize teeth were sunk deep into the girl's neck. When Cassie gasped aloud, he looked up. For a moment, his inflamed eyes looked startled but then he relaxed and his bloodied mouth grinned at her.

Horrified, Cassie shot round to the other side. Yet the girl was still wearing her distant smile. With both of her hands covering her mouth, Cassie watched the colour drain from Taslima's gorgeous brown face. It turned red and warped uncannily into Bernie's burnt features. In seconds, the complexion paled to pink and took on Cassie's appearance. The sickly metamorphosis was complete when the face bleached to white and mutated into the girl in the car crash. Wilting in her boyfriend's arms, her head flopped uselessly on to his shoulder like a deflated balloon. But he'd had his fill of her. He threw the empty shell to one side and strode away.

Tentatively, Cassie walked to the discarded remains and knelt down. There was nothing but the yellow dress and a mask. When Cassie took the face-mask in both hands, she felt a warm glow spreading throughout her body, an unexpected tingle of pleasure. The texture of the mask was soft like silk and the intricate lifelike features were strangely gratifying.

"Hello, Cassie. You look a bit calmer this time. How are you feeling?"

Her eye was half open. Through the haze she saw Dr Staunton. She tried to ask something but her mouth felt detached from her desire to speak. She stuttered and cursed herself. Her out-of-control lips quivered and slavered. Yet she was not going to give up. In a barely audible voice, she mumbled, "Sore." It was a pathetic performance but at least the word didn't come out as *shore*. Even though she still couldn't speak properly, her mouth now felt cumbersome and unwilling rather than incomplete and incapable.

"That's as I'd expect. It doesn't mean anything's wrong."

"How am I?"

"Pardon?"

Cassie took a deep breath and tried again. "How am I?"

"I'm pleased, Cassie. You're going to be fine. Beautiful, I'd say."

Before the surgeon had finished, Cassie drifted off again. She was peaceful, though, as if the last word she'd heard – "beautiful" – had soothed her to sleep.

An hour later, she woke and carried on the conversation

as if scant seconds had passed. "Going to be?" Her voice sounded like an incompetent ventriloquist's.

Dr Staunton was taking photographs of her patient's face from different angles. She put down the camera and drew up the chair. "You're doing great, Cassie, because I didn't think you'd be able to speak at all at this stage. But you're going to have to say that again. Sorry."

"*Going* to be fine, you said."

"Yes."

"Not fine now," Cassie struggled to splutter.

"You're still in transition. You've got severe bruising – that's expected after what I've done to you. And there's your stitches and dressings. But . . . you're complete. It'll heal. I think you're going to like what you see."

Inside, Cassie was panicking. "See now?"

"Oh, I think you could leave it for a couple of days before you take a look. I'm not trying to hide anything from you – not at all – but you'll be stronger then and some of the swelling will have gone down a bit."

Cassie breathed a sigh of relief. She would not have dared to look into a mirror. She just knew that some things in life would make her close her eyes: an assassin putting a gun against her head, being on a plane about to crash-land. She wouldn't have a choice. Consumed by terror, instinct would take control and the shutter would come down involuntarily. It was exactly the same with a new face. She was afraid of what she would see, and who she would see.

In the private recovery room, Dr Staunton reassured her patient, "You've got the anti-rejection drug in your drip at the moment. And painkillers, but I doubt if they're deadening every single ache."

"No."

"The physio's going well, though." Seeing her patient's unfavourable reaction, Dr Staunton added with a smile, "Your frown proves it. Very expressive. Your muscle control is coming on leaps and bounds. Maybe it's not as fast as you want but it's far better than I thought it would be. You've only had a couple of sessions and I don't need a translator any more. And you're beginning to develop a lovely smile. We've just got to give you more reasons to practise it."

Cassie did not respond.

"Cassie, I think it's time. . ."

"No."

"You're not mended – by any stretch of the imagination – but why not?"

"I can't look!" Cassie cried.

"You can. I think you'll like what you're becoming."

"I can't! I'm not ready."

"It's difficult, I know."

Cassie looked away and muttered, "I'm scared."

"I understand. But believe me, everything's going to be fine." Deciding on a gently playful style, Dr Staunton added, "I have to admit you look like you've gone a few rounds with the world champ but you can look beyond the cuts and bruises."

"No."

From outside in the general ward came the muffled sound of a folk singer, voice and accordion.

"More stupid music," Cassie muttered.

Dr Staunton smiled wryly. "You'd be amazed. Exposing patients to music and works of art cuts down on the need for post-operative antidepressants and painkillers. While there's music, no one thinks about aches, pains and anxieties, they escape into their imaginations for a bit. Can't be bad."

Cassie didn't reply. She realized that Dr Staunton was eager to show off her transplant handiwork but it was incredibly daunting for Cassie. When the acid first went about its work, Cassie needed to see. She was prepared to confront her wounds because it was still her own face. Now the surgeon had got to work on her, she couldn't bear to look because it would be someone else in the mirror. She'd be gazing upon the risen dead.

"So, what do you want to do, Cassie?" asked Dr Staunton. "You've got to look sometime."

Cassie shrugged.

"Would the counsellor help?"

"No." Suddenly, Cassie had a bright idea, a way forward that she could endure. She said, "I want Wayne."

Hilary Staunton was taken aback. "What? Wayne Wingate?"

Cassie nodded gently, not straining her tender head.

"But he's. . ." Hilary decided not to continue her protest. "Why?"

"He's honest."

"What?"

"I want him to look," she replied slowly, grappling with an uncooperative mouth, "and tell me what he thinks."

Dr Staunton said, "But does it matter what he thinks? Isn't it more important what you think?"

"Yes, but . . . I need him."

Hilary took a deep breath. "Well, it's not what I'd recommend."

"I want Wayne."

"Are you absolutely sure?"

"Yes."

Reluctantly, Dr Staunton said, "OK, Cassie. But first, I'll have to consult Professor Clayton. If Wayne's got any sort of infection, I won't let him anywhere near you, not till you're much further down the road to recovery."

GLASS 11

The six Catholic girls had got hold of Jane, a lone Protestant. There was little in this world more cruel and bitchy than a group of like-minded girls who'd got their hands on the odd-one-out. They had pinned her down on the ground. Someone had her palm pressed firmly over Jane's mouth so she couldn't cry out. The others were painting the Irish flag – green, white and gold rectangles – on her cheeks, bare midriff, arms and legs. There were giggles, laughs, sarcastic comments about fat Protestant slags.

Cassie had never lacked courage or compassion. When she saw what was going on, she waded straight in. "Oi!" Yanking girls off Jane, Cassie got to the centre of the spitefulness and broke it up. "You're horrible!" she cried, helping the Protestant to her feet. Then she stood to one side as Jane ran away without a word. Not a word of thanks, of course. Cassie didn't expect it. She had never lacked a sense of realism either. While she saw Jane as a human being first and a Protestant second, Jane would never see anything in Cassie apart from her religion. She knew that the next day Jane might throw a stone at her because she was Catholic and any Catholic was to be despised.

Now, Cassie tried to rediscover that courage.

The first head to appear round the door was Dr Staunton's. "Is your mind still made up?"

"Yes," Cassie answered.

"How about now, then? Shall I let Wayne in? He's here."

Cassie inhaled deeply to steel herself. "Yes."

"All right." The surgeon held the door open for Wayne and, when he passed her, she gave him a look that should have reminded him what she'd said about being diplomatic.

Wayne approached Cassie's bed and uttered, "Wow."

"What?"

He'd already forgotten Dr Staunton's lecture. "You're just like that guy in the Texas Chainsaw Massacre."

"What!"

"Don't take it bad. It's all . . . puffed up. Like you're wearing someone else's skin."

Dr Staunton's worst fears were coming true. She was about to intervene when Wayne recouped the situation.

He added, "But it's gonna be good when it's back to normal."

"Why go 'Wow'?" asked Cassie.

Embarrassed, Wayne dropped his eyes. "Sure, it looks like you've been slashed but it's much better than before. When you've grown your hair at the front you'll be right hot."

"Really?"

"Your eyes, nose and mouth are blotchy – black and blue – but they're all there."

In her first upheaval, Cassie had changed her name and home. She'd been forced to leave behind friends like Bernie. She'd sworn on a bible never to tell anyone, not even Bernie, her new name, address and identity. As Cassie

O'Rourke, she'd sworn never to contact any of her old friends. In this second upheaval, she'd been forced to leave behind her appearance. From Cassie's point of view, there was nothing left of her external self. It had all been stripped away. Her name, her old life and friends, her family, her home, and now her face completed the transformation. Three things remained from her past life: a photograph of how she used to look, memories, and a father who would appear suddenly, profess to love her, and disappear again. Wrestling with the muscles of her face, she glanced at Wayne and said, "You saw my photo. Do I look like . . . me?"

"A bit, yeah. And a bit like the one with the earrings. Maybe better than both."

Dr Staunton breathed a sigh of relief. The loose cannon seemed to be firing in the right direction now. He was also providing her patient with an incentive to speak. The best physiotherapy for Cassie was simply talking, interacting, exercising those facial muscles. "I'll leave you two for a while. All right?"

Cassie and Wayne both nodded, pleased to be rid of the adult spectator.

"You want me to stay?" Wayne asked.

Cassie looked at him and said, "Do you want to?"

"Suppose," Wayne replied. He thought for a few seconds and then added, "Anything to get away from the noise."

"Noise?"

Wayne nodded towards the door and the unseen folk singer beyond. "Not exactly chart material out there."

"How are *you* doing?"

Wayne didn't quite catch her faltering words. He had to concentrate to understand her. "What?"

"How are you getting on?"

"I'm all done. The professor bloke's doing millions of tests but I'm great. I used to be bad every day. Not all day, like, just sometime in the day I'd get foggy in the brain, cramps, horribly thirsty. Not now. I could run a marathon. I'm the world's first robot-controlled boy." He beamed with pleasure and pride.

"Good." Cassie thought of herself as the world's first chameleon-girl but she didn't say anything. Besides, with her slovenly mouth, she couldn't possibly pronounce *chameleon*.

In an awkward silence, Wayne looked enviously round the room. Then he said, "Hey, this is all right. You're lucky."

Cassie wasn't thinking about the room. She was still wondering how much courage she could summon. "Wayne, have you got a mirror?"

"What?"

"A mirror. Have you got one?"

"No. But I can get one. Is that what you want? No problem."

"I don't know. Er . . . maybe. Yes, I think so."

Reaching for the door handle, he said, "I'll be a couple of seconds."

A few minutes later, Wayne had the opportunity to prove that the secret code was 1987. Tapping it into the keypad by Cassie's room while no one was looking, he sneaked back inside and handed her a small make-up mirror.

Cassie avoided looking into it. Pensively, she held the

mirror in her bandaged hand so that its back was towards her. "Is this yours?" she asked. Her face tried to crease up but managed only a meaningless twitch.

"It's yours now."

Suspicious, she said, "Where did you get it?"

"There's this old woman, she used to be yellow but she's got a pig kidney now and she's gone normal."

Cassie thought for a moment before replying, "She won't know she's changed."

"How's that?"

"You've nicked her mirror."

"You need it," Wayne said. To him, that seemed to be a perfectly satisfactory and sensible justification of the theft.

Cassie shook her head. "You take it back when I'm done."

He shrugged. "OK." Then he watched her as she fiddled with the mirror but made no attempt to use it. "Is this your first look?" he asked.

Cassie nodded.

Wayne didn't understand what was holding her back. Her face was pretty much wrecked before and now it was just beaten up. OK, it was oddly fixed like a mask and, when she wanted to change the direction of her gaze, she shifted her whole head rather than swivel her eye. But sometimes she managed some sort of expression. "Is it a big deal?"

"Very. I've just hijacked another girl's identity and lost my own." She nearly added, "Again," but stopped herself.

"Just look and get it over with, like."

"Easier said than done."

"Sorry?"

Her disjointed slur infuriated her. "Easy for you to say."

Wayne smiled proudly. "In at the deep end, me."

What made her who she was? Her brain, her soul and her appearance. Changing her appearance changed *her*. That was a third of herself, gone. Was it any wonder that she was terrified? She feared that the ghoul had been replaced by a female version of Frankenstein's creature.

"It's simple," Wayne said. "Before, you were grotty. Now you're gonna be fine."

Cassie had never been entirely happy with her looks. She liked to think she wasn't the fussy sort but her cheeks had been too podgy, her eyes weren't large enough, her nose was too long and her lips were too thin. She ought be delighted to try another face. As if her hand were fighting against immense pressure, she pulled the mirror closer.

When the battered street fighter came into focus, she gasped. It was nothing like herself. Transfixed by the image in the glass, she stroked the foreign blotchy skin on the cheeks with her fingertips protruding from the bandages. She shivered. It was like touching someone else, a long-lost sister perhaps. Vaguely similar but definitely different. It was a sinister feeling but her overwhelming emotion was relief.

That dreadful mangled blob had gone from the centre of her face. In its place was a homely nose that looked just like her own. She couldn't see anything with the left eye, of course, but it looked absolutely normal. No one would know she was partly blind. She could barely bat the eyelids but at least they were both in place. The folds of skin around the eyes were inflamed. The eyebrows were agreeably arched, though, even if the skin looked baggy. Covering her teeth and gums, the lips were nice and full but they were also tinged with blue bruising. There was an ugly gash that ran over the shaven part of her head and down beside each ear like a thin hairband encrusted with rubies. She had exchanged one set of stains for another.

And despite everything, her tear ducts were fully functioning yet again.

"What's wrong? Why are you crying?"

"I don't know," she whimpered.

Of course she knew. And she wished that Wayne could figure it out without asking. It was because her life had been turned upside down. She'd had too much bad news, too much hurt, and now the good news was too much as well.

12 GLUE

The cuts and bruises were healing remarkably quickly. No sign of infection. Cassie remained emotional but she was also resilient. An ideal specimen for Dr Staunton's first experiment.

Once Cassie had got used to seeing the girl in the mirror, the physiotherapist placed her in front of a video screen every day to train her to pull a hundred faces. "Did you know," he said without warning, "the government's scrapped GCSEs."

"What?"

"That's it!" he cried. "Watch the monitor. See, your eyebrows went up and your mouth opened. That's a beautiful expression of surprise. And a fully articulated 'What?' If this was a GCSE, you'd have just got an A."

It was true that, little by little, she was getting control over the facial muscles. She didn't know how long it would take before they felt like *her* facial muscles, though. She realized that her speech had improved because she no longer had to put up with a stream of "Pardon?", "Sorry?", "What?" from anyone who spoke to her. She still stumbled over a lot of words but at least she was intelligible.

"And people will love you for your smile. Deep, prominent lines down your cheeks, curving round the ends of your lips."

At once Cassie looked worried and suspicious.

"No. Natural lines," the physiotherapist reassured her. "It's a gorgeous smile." He paused and then asked, "Do you like cabbage?"

"No," she answered with a cast-iron expression.

"OK. Let's work on this one. The classic turning-up-the-nose-at-the-mention-of-cabbage-or-spiders. It's a tricky one, this grimace. Lots of nose, cheek and upper lip movement."

Each morning, just before she cleaned her teeth gingerly and showered, Cassie undertook a thorough inspection of the face in the bathroom mirror. It was as if she still couldn't believe it. Some of the scabs along her cut-here line were beginning to fall away, leaving a narrow track of smooth skin that was slightly paler than the surrounding tissue. But only Cassie's critical eye would spot it. The join high on her forehead was becoming obscured by fine spiky hair. The real reason she peered so closely into the mirror was lack of confidence. With a tightness in her stomach, she was searching for signs that the face was becoming detached. She didn't know what she'd see but she recalled a collage she'd made out of pieces of paper in an art lesson years ago. It was a beautiful piece but she'd used the wrong sort of glue. The edges of the paper became unstuck and curled up, ruining its appearance. Every time she walked towards a mirror an image of that sad collage came unbidden to her mind.

She was fully established on her little green anti-rejection pills and she was taking meals tentatively but normally. It felt less like chaotic feeding time at the zoo and she no longer sent people away so they wouldn't see the unappetizing sight of her eating. Her father had come and gone. Fully briefed by Dr Staunton, he'd declared himself to be delighted because he had regained a dazzling daughter. Cassie had got in only one question. "Doesn't it bother you that I've changed?"

"See that nurse over there, changing the picture?"

"Paintings appear, disappear and reappear in different places. Art's supposed to cheer us up – like the music," Cassie had explained.

"Well, she's taken down a nice one, left a mess, and covered it up with a better one." All trace of O'Rourke's Irish accent had been trained out of him. He'd looked into his daughter's face and said, "It bothered me to see you how you were – but now I think you're even prettier than you were before the acid."

Cassie knew it. She could see it for herself and she was grateful but, when she fingered the skin, it still felt as if she were touching a friend's face. When her dad leaned forward and kissed her on the cheek, she sensed his lips. The kiss belonged to her but it was filtered through someone else's skin as if delivered by proxy.

At once, O'Rourke's bodyguards had whisked him away to a safe house in a secret location.

It was straight after his visit that Dr Staunton and Professor Clayton gathered together with Wayne in Cassie's room and first raised the possibility of their own safe house nearby in Sheffield, funded jointly by the Department of Experimental Medicine, the Social Services, Cassie's father and the police.

*

The woman who was ushered discreetly into Cassie's room was scary. The skin of her face had been stretched so tight by a series of facelifts that she looked permanently startled. Her eyes stared out of skin as smooth and taut as a balloon on the point of bursting. Her appearance reminded Cassie of a joke she'd once heard and she couldn't help but speculate what would happen if one of the woman's cheeks suffered a pinprick. No wonder she was locked into a stunned expression. Her lips were glossed heavily in bright red. The jet-black of her long witch-like hair had come out of a bottle and, no doubt, covered copious quantities of grey. The colour matched her extravagant eyelashes, coated in mascara.

Cassie wasn't in the mood for jokes. She felt sick. This woman, probably in her seventies, must believe that a lack of wrinkles made her appear young when really she looked utterly absurd. There were more realistic faces in waxworks. Cassie was almost surprised when she spoke. Her lips had been pinned back so forcefully that it was a wonder she could utter anything.

"So," she said in a syrupy voice, "you're Cassie, the miracle girl."

Cassie tried out her newly recovered ability to frown. "Cassie, yes."

"Come over to the light and let me have a good look at you, honey."

Behind the zombie, Dr Staunton nodded at Cassie.

By the table light, the woman muttered, "That's right. Just here." Invading Cassie's personal space, she began to study her face like a forensic scientist looking for

81

microscopic clues. "You're lovely, Cassie. Ah, to be your age again. Such skin."

Cassie stood rigidly to attention, tense under the unwelcome examination.

"And how do you think your operation's turned out, honey?" Her knuckles brushed against the skin between Cassie's ear and mouth.

Cassie waited for the woman's fingers to move softly across the lips before she spoke. "I'm. . . Well, it's hard to come to terms with but I've got to be pleased. I had nothing after . . . the accident and now everyone says I look really good."

"They're not kidding." Viewing Cassie from the side, she added, "I saw the photographs. Poor you. But now look at you! You'll break boys' hearts." Plainly, the woman was getting carried away. "And you're speaking so well already." She ran her hand through the fine hair growing over Cassie's forehead. "Give me a smile, honey. Indulge an old lady."

Cassie tried not to cringe. Her smiles were still timid and the one she managed for her guest was very tentative. It was like saying cheese for a photographer when she felt anything but cheerful. Perhaps, though, to a sad old lady whose smile resembled a vampire's, Cassie's effort would be angelic.

"Mmm. They're right. Charming." She walked right around Cassie like she might walk round a model wearing a coat that she was thinking of buying. She dipped down to look up at Cassie's neck and chin and then said to Dr Staunton, "This is wonderful work. Such a doll."

Cassie would have thought her visitor was far more like

an inanimate doll than she was herself. And she didn't enjoy being treated like a commodity.

"I'm convinced already," the woman announced. Turning back to Cassie, she said, "You're so lucky. The young heal quickly. It would take me a lot longer. Still. . ." Her voice disappeared into a contented sigh. She could not resist touching Cassie's new face again. This time her fingertips explored the forehead and she quivered as if she were experiencing sexual pleasure. "Absolutely gorgeous. You look after yourself, honey. You hear me?"

"Yes."

As the woman swept out of the room, Dr Staunton nodded her thanks in Cassie's direction. The surgeon's face beamed with pride and satisfaction. Self-satisfaction probably.

This time, it was Wayne who identified the visitor. "Yeah, I saw her," he said with his usual indifference. "Couldn't miss her, like."

"I wonder who she was."

"I were throwing a wobbly in case she stopped and warbled at us. She was a singer in the 1960s or sometime."

Cassie practised shock. "Oh? How do you know?"

"My auntie's into that sort of thing." He snorted, making his disdain clear. "She's got truckloads of records from the dark ages. First one, first pile, has got your friend on the cover."

"Sure?"

"She's younger, not so creepy, but yeah." He closed his eyes for a moment. "I can picture it. Name of Dorothy Something-or-other."

"How many visitors have *you* been shown to?" asked Cassie.

"Hundreds."

"Hundreds?"

"I don't know. A few, like."

"All old?"

"Ancient."

Cassie nodded. To her, it was obvious what was going on but she didn't understand Wayne's role. Clearly, she had become a model – an advert – for a cosmetic treatment on offer in the Department of Experimental Medicine. A transplant was the ultimate hi-tech facelift and it was probably very expensive. But why was Wayne on show as well? What could he advertise? It was unlikely that every one of his wealthy visitors was diabetic and there was nothing to see but a healthy boy. She began to wonder if there was more to his treatment than he'd been told.

And Cassie was curious about the elderly celebrities who saw the result of her operation. Would they really go ahead with horrific surgery just to acquire the appearance of their choice? Presumably, their quest for good looks overcame any squeamishness. It made Cassie shudder to think that, at the whim of crazy people like Dorothy, a market for young faces might emerge. If the transplant procedure was successful, if they had enough money to pay for it, who would decide the value of a young face? Presumably some faces would be more desirable and more costly than others. Cassie imagined a macabre and tasteless auction of a particularly fine face. Already football managers haggled among themselves to pay millions for a top-class player. Perhaps the rich would hold a similar degrading competition for a top-class face.

"What's with this safe house, do you reckon?" Wayne said, interrupting her daydream.

"They want to free our beds but keep us handy for check-ups." She swallowed, trying to relax her mouth before she continued. "And we'll be on call to tell people about our treatments."

"But why are the feds throwing money at it? I bet they're keeping tabs on me."

"The feds?"

"Police."

Cassie's smile was evolving nicely. "I don't think it's got much to do with you."

"Uh?"

"I bet it's a house with a panic button. Chipping in for one of those is cheap compared to paying for a 24-hour bodyguard."

"Who wants a bodyguard?"

"It's not a case of wanting," Cassie replied. "I don't get a choice."

"You? The bouncer's for you? Why?"

"I'm not allowed to talk about it."

"Why not?"

Cassie shrugged helplessly and wiped her tired mouth.

Easily sidetracked, Wayne glanced at the array of pills on Cassie's bedside cabinet. Poking at them, he asked, "What's those? The green ones."

"They're important. Anti-rejection tablets."

"Ugh, rejecting a face! Disgusting." Looking back at the tablets, he said, "These?"

"Antidepressants."

"Why do you take them?"

"They give them to everyone who has recon. . ." She broke off, annoyed that she couldn't manage to say reconstructive surgery. "They're to keep my spirits up."

"And the yellow ones?"

"I'm supposed to call them MDMA but they're ecstasy."

"Ecstasy? You could sell them," Wayne said enthusiastically, picking one up and staring at it.

"They help people get over their. . ." Cassie paused but was determined to spit out a difficult word, "Trauma."

"Trauma? What's that?"

"Shock, fear."

"What shock?"

"The acid, the transplant and . . . the thing I can't talk about."

"Do they work?"

Cassie shrugged. "Not a lot."

"You'd do better by going clubbing with them."

"I'd need some persuading I want to go clubbing at the moment." Then, desperate to forget her meeting with Dorothy, Cassie added with a smile, "Hey, what did the inflatable teacher say to the naughty inflatable student who brought a needle into the inflatable school?"

Wayne could watch that smile all day. Distracted, he said, "What's inflatable?"

Cassie shook her head. "Boy, you know how to ruin a good joke." Anyway, her heart wasn't really in it.

BONE 13

Soon to be Professor Staunton, Hilary had carried out Cassie O'Rourke's face transplant for three reasons. She did it not only to help Cassie – to make her feel better about herself – but also to make Cassie easier on the eye for everyone else. She needed a recuperating patient to sway her wealthy sponsors. And not least, Hilary had to prove she had the skills to accomplish a face transplant before anyone else. Doing it before any male surgeons would be the icing on her cake.

Writing up her work in the coffee room, Hilary's fingers were flying across the keypad.

The world's first complete face transplant has been performed using (i) advanced microsurgical techniques and (ii) a novel and highly effective immunosuppressive drug that also aids nerve regeneration. The success of the operation signals a new era in transplant medicine.

(i) In recent years, severed fingers, hands, arms and penises have all been replaced through modern microsurgery, with varying degrees of success. Improvements in microsurgical methods have now allowed an entire face to be given to a young female recipient.

(ii) Limb transplants have been carried out in several

different countries with mixed results. The procedure is held back because foreign skin remains the most readily rejected tissue and because nerve repair is difficult. A newly developed tolerance therapy opens up life-saving transplant techniques and reconstructive surgery by preventing rejection of foreign skin and aiding nerve regeneration.

When Richard strode into the rest room, he said, "Hilary. I see you've installed someone in Room 21, away from prying eyes."

She stopped typing and looked up. "My next face transplant. Remember? I mentioned him in my last talk. Rather different from Cassie: male, 67 years old. A large tumour's demolished the left side of his face."

Richard poured himself a fresh coffee. "So you've got to do some grafting of bone as well this time."

"Yeah. Quite a challenge."

"Have you got a matched donor?"

"There's more choice of corpses with a 67 year old than a teenager. The lights have just turned green."

"How much did you have to pay?"

Hilary had been lucky this time. Of two good matches, one was an anonymous asylum seeker, knocked down by a train, and the other had two greedy sons who would have welcomed an offer for their father's face. Hilary had not needed to get involved in a sordid deal because the nameless immigrant turned out to be the more compatible and acceptable to her patient. "A box of chocolates for the coroner. That's it."

Richard looked away in disgust. "And what safeguards are in place," he asked, "to make sure the donor's really dead?"

"There's a code of practice. Two independent doctors have got to certify a potential donor's brain-dead before any organ or tissue's removed."

"That's supposed to stop accidents and corruption, is it?"

"Yes."

Richard shook his head cynically. "How's it going with Cassie?"

"Physically, it's beautiful," Hilary answered. "She's set a cracking pace for healing, nerve growth and muscle control. Her neurons have grown brilliantly into the transplanted nerves. Psychologically, it was touch and go for a while but she's becoming emotionally attached to the face now."

"I suppose if there's no emotional bond, you can get a physical breakdown."

"Exactly," said Hilary. "But all her guilt about stealing someone else's face is outweighed by the idea of being attractive. She's a canny girl and she knows the value of looking good."

"Now you're tackling an old man so you've got a male advert for your sponsors."

"No," Hilary replied firmly. "You go and examine him and you'll see why I want to help."

Plonking himself down in a chair, Richard said with obvious distaste, "Have you planned a purely cosmetic op yet?"

"No, but I've got three in the pipeline. All of them were very impressed with Cassie's appearance."

"I hate this surgical showmanship."

Hilary said, "Yes, but you'd be amazed what they're willing to pay. And my immunosuppressant is going to sell by the spadeful. The proceeds will run my research for years."

"Let me guess. Your celebs are all waiting for donors that're a lot less than 67."

"The way they see it, there's no point turning the clock back a bit. They're looking for a sizeable rewind. They get so down if they don't look wonderful."

Richard let out a weary breath.

Hilary continued, "It'd be great if we lived in some Utopia where everyone celebrates everyone else's appearance but we don't. We live in an unfair society where the attractive get on better than the ugly. Let's be blunt. If you're going to sack someone, do you make it the old hag or the attractive young woman? It's called prejudice and I wish it didn't happen but it does. You and me, we live in the real world."

Richard couldn't criticize any more, not when he was beginning to benefit by the same clients and the same logic.

"Do you know the statistics, Richard?" Hilary asked. "This year, two million people in America and Europe will go voluntarily under the knife to have their flesh carved open and manipulated to improve their appearance. Brits alone will spend nearly two hundred million pounds on transforming themselves. Mostly it'll be women, with breasts, buttocks and faces – particularly noses – at the top of the list. They all want to be Barbie or Lara Croft. That's a lot of customers who'll help to fund the work I'm going to do for free on the poor man in Room 21. Poor in both senses: he's unfortunate and skint. With people like him needing my attention, you're not going to make me feel guilty about cosmetic treatment so don't bother trying." With that, she turned her attention back to her laptop.

14 ECSTASY

In the compact living room of the terraced house, Wayne spread out his arms and spun around. "This is brilliant!" he declared. "My own place. Free."

"Mine too," Cassie reminded him.

"Yeah, great." It *was* great. He was shacked up in Hillsborough with a girl who'd changed from ugly duckling to magnificent swan. He was fit, she was gorgeous, and they were both out of range of parents and guardians. Life didn't get much better than that.

The house was owned by the university and usually it was let each year to a couple of students. To become the new lodgers, Cassie and Wayne had to pay a few penalties. They had to accept daily supervision by someone from Sheffield Social Services. That was normal for Cassie, who was used to living in a hostel run by the Social Services in Belfast. They were required to have an alarm that would bring medics, the police or both rushing to the house in any emergency. They'd be enrolled at the local comprehensive and they had to agree to twice-weekly visits from a tutor throughout August to bring them back up to speed in time for the new term. Just because they'd been discharged from the ward, it didn't mean their treatments were over. Cassie had to get on the tram and go into the Department of Experimental Medicine three times a week for physiotherapy and check-ups. On one of those visits, she had to drag Wayne in as well. For the sake of their well-being, frequent assessments were essential. Occasionally, they'd be asked to entertain hospital visitors as well.

For the first time in ages, Cassie laughed. The sound could have been mistaken for the clearing of a throat but Wayne recognized it for what it was. When Cassie saw him looking puzzled, she explained, "We're guinea pigs in a cage but at least we can play spot-the-celebrity. Cher, Michael Jackson, who knows? Just think. We might get more stars than the Odeon."

"Yeah," Wayne agreed. "That'd make us right famous as well. We might get gangsters on the run, wanting to change their faces, or undercover feds not wanting to be recognized."

Of course, he was getting carried away but Cassie didn't comment because he was too close for comfort. She changed the subject. "Are you going to your uncle's to get your things?"

"Tomorrow. What about yours?"

"Social Services in Northern Ireland are sending them over, apparently." At long last, Cassie was feeling good. She could say *social services* with confidence, almost perfectly. Her accent had returned, her pronunciation caused no embarrassment and only a few awkward words triggered frustration. She'd had her hair cut short so that the newly grown stuff did not look out of place. She really liked what she saw in the mirror now. "All right if I have the front bedroom?" She wanted the comfort of a streetlight, just like her room when she lived with her parents and brothers.

Wayne shrugged. "Suppose." It would be too optimistic, he knew, for her to suggest that they share the same one. Anyway, the beds were incredibly narrow.

Hinting, Cassie said, "Who's going to put the kettle on?"

"You don't drink tea or coffee, do you? Yuck."

"Tea, yes. Coffee, no. You know how to make tea, though?"

"Not really."

Cassie sighed. "I bet I'm going to have to teach you a few things. Do you know how to use a washing machine?"

Wayne shook his head.

"An oven?"

"No."

"Not everything in this world gets done by robots, you know. Any chance you'd recognize a vacuum cleaner?"

"It's a bit strange about your nanorobots, isn't it?" said Cassie.

"Is it?"

"Well, they're sorting out your diabetes, aren't they?"

"Doing a good job," Wayne replied.

"Why have you got to have fitness tests and whole-body scans, then?"

Wayne shrugged, not really caring.

"Why does the hospital keep showing you to old people?"

"Dunno."

"They can't all be diabetic. There's something funny going on."

"Is there?"

"With me, there's a face to look at," Cassie explained.

94

"With you, there's nothing. Just invisible robots on the inside."

Wayne fell silent for a while, then, looking stunned, he said, "You don't think they're eyeing my face, do you? They're not going to cut it off and give it to some old bloke?"

Cassie smiled. "You'd have to be dead for that."

"You don't think they're going to kill me?"

"No, Wayne. There's a law against that sort of thing. Besides, haven't you been shown to some women as well?"

"Yes."

"Well, I don't think they're after your face," said Cassie.

"Phew."

"I was just wondering. . ."

"What?" Wayne said, still nervy.

"Well, perhaps these robots do more than fix your diabetes."

"Yeah? Like what?"

Cassie shrugged. "I don't know. Old people are interested in me because they want young faces. Extreme cosmetic surgery. They must be looking at you for something similar. Like, your nanorobots keep you young and fit or something."

"Really?"

"Maybe I'm wrong but it'd explain the fitness tests and stuff."

Brightening, Wayne said, "You mean I'll be young for ever? Great!"

Cassie sighed, wondering if she could find a purpose for his ability to gallop away with an idea. "If I showed you an iron, would you go full steam ahead with that as well?"

"Uh?"

"Never mind."

Fascinated, Wayne had gone back to the idea of face donors. "They could hire a hit-man to kill real lookers without spoiling their faces. Or they could dig up dead bodies before they go off."

"Wayne."

"Yes?"

"Come off it. This is the twenty-first century. The worst they're going to do is bribe relatives to buy bodies of people who've died. That's bad enough."

Unperturbed, Wayne shrugged. "Dead people don't need faces."

Cassie did not respond because she felt torn. She'd been taught that a human body was a temple of the Holy Spirit yet she'd benefited from the desecration of one poor girl. She could think of several other reasons why the church would condemn what she'd done. Most had something to do with vanity. There again, it was ages since she'd been a good Catholic girl. When God abandoned her mother and brothers, she'd abandoned His church.

"All these rich greys that're going to have transplants!" With his usual amount of tact, Wayne said, "Just imagine if one of them rejected a face. What a mess!" The thought made him grimace and then smile broadly.

"Yes," Cassie replied, "the result would be almost as gruesome as nanorobots going mad and eating away an entire brain, leaving a complete moron."

It was the first game of the new season. The enthusiasm

96

and hope of the Wednesday fans had not yet been dulled by the first few results. In high spirits, the supporters emerged from the estates, buses and trams, converging noisily on Middlewood Road.

Down at the Hillsborough shops, Wayne cheered and waved, joining in the fun. Cassie shrank back from the crowds, the police and their dogs, and felt her heart go into overdrive. As the anxiety attack took hold of her, she struggled to breathe. She wanted to alert Wayne that something was wrong but she couldn't utter a word. Gripped by fear, she struggled to remain on her feet.

The can flew high over the police officers' heads, over their horses, and plunged down on Cassie. With her one eye, she was unable to judge its trajectory and could not get out of its way. She screamed and clutched at her forehead. It wasn't pain that made her cry out but the shock. Immediately, her mind turned to the acid bomb but the liquid that was trickling into her short mousy hair, down her face and on to her hands didn't feel corrosive. It was sticky and smelly. But the damage had already been done. Not physical damage this time. Overcome by terror, she screamed again. Her howl silenced the crowd with its intensity.

For once, Wayne was startled into accepting his responsibility. He grabbed hold of Cassie, trying to steady her. It didn't work and they tumbled together on to the pavement. Cassie was clawing at her face, threatening to damage it, so he grasped her wrists and pulled her hands away. He glanced at the can in the gutter and then smelled the liquid on her cheeks. "It's all right!" he shouted at her. "It's beer, only beer."

97

The next thing he knew he was being lifted from Cassie by strong arms. He was back on his feet, held by one huge fed behind him, facing another. "No!" he cried, desperate to break free and help his friend.

"What's going on?"

He tried to wriggle out of the officer's grip. "Let me go, stupid! You don't understand. She's in trouble."

"Oh yes?" the policeman said. "What kind of trouble?"

The fogginess in Wayne's brain was nothing to do with diabetes this time. He said, "I don't think the ecstasy's working."

Immediately the fed nodded knowingly. "Ecstasy, eh? I see."

"No!" Wayne shrieked. "I mean. . ."

But it was too late. The feds had come to a conclusion.

As they dragged Wayne away, he cried, "You've got to get her to. . ."

It was no use. A policewoman was kneeling beside Cassie and another was on the radio. Neither took any notice of Wayne.

FIRE 15

From that moment, Wayne realized that it was going to be hard to be Cassie's friend. He also realized that's exactly what he was determined to be. Even though he felt helpless, he refused to cave in to the police machine. He refused to be arrested quietly. He tried over and over again to explain, and no matter how many times he got an unbelieving, "Oh yes?" as a response, no matter how maddening it was, he tried again.

It was the police doctor who remembered Wayne as a diabetic. The tag around his neck confirmed it. The doctor also recognized the classic symptoms of hypoglycaemia. The boy was confused, shaking, sweaty, restless, almost hysterical. At once, the doctor ordered a sweet drink and sugar to pull him out of his hypo. Then he called Dr Flint at the hospital. But Dr Flint was perplexed and concerned. He suggested a call to Professor Richard Clayton at the hospital's Department of Experimental Medicine. . .

Cassie was back in a private room. She was flat out in bed, chemically stabilized and subdued. When her one good eye was directed at Wayne, he wasn't sure if she was looking at him or through him.

Wayne just sat there. He was trying to figure out a strange sensation that he had never experienced before. Whatever it was, it meant he was happy to wait at this girl's bedside without getting bored. It meant he was anxious about a fellow human being for the first time in his life. He was also trying to figure out the name of that animal – a lizard type of thing. It could change its appearance or something like. Anyway, that was his flatmate – only nicer-looking now.

Without warning, Cassie turned her head towards him. "I think I brought the acid attack on myself."

Wayne turned round in case she was speaking to someone behind him, someone who knew what she was talking about, but no one was there.

"I swore on a bible but, after Mum and the boys, the bible meant nothing to me. You can't just leave your best friend behind without a word. I said I wouldn't call Bernie but I had to. I told her I was going to Belfast to be Cassie. I knew she wouldn't tell anyone else but. . ."

Wayne watched her weeping, not realizing that he was holding her hand. He still wasn't sure that she was really speaking to him. She could be imagining he was someone else or maybe she was talking to herself. He certainly couldn't make much sense of it.

"I read about her in the paper. No one knew if it was sectarian violence or a Catholic punishment beating. More than a beating. I think it was the bad guys. They poured petrol over her. They tortured the information out of her. And when they got it, they set fire to her anyway. Imagine what she went through. She died and it was my fault."

Wayne had never seen anything like it. He didn't know one person could produce so many tears, like water streaming out of a crushed sponge. He had no idea what to do but, for some reason, he didn't call for a nurse. He thought Cassie wouldn't want any more of an audience. It was debatable whether she even knew that she already had an audience for her confession.

"It's all about Dad," she said. "He hated the men of violence – the bad guys. Because he was a Catholic, he was ideal for the police. He went undercover into the IFG and got lots of intelligence out – till they realized he was leaking information." She paused and swallowed, her head flopping to one side through tiredness or despair. "When they're betrayed, the men in balaclavas are absolutely ruthless and totally unforgiving. Even now. The peace process doesn't stretch to police informants." She wiped away the moisture from her nose, mouth and cheeks with one hand and squeezed Wayne's relentlessly with the other. "The bad guys vowed to destroy us. Not just Dad. The whole family. They got Mum and the boys at home with a nail bomb. Dad and me, we felt so guilty, especially Dad. He'd gone out to the shops and I was late back from school, fooling around with Bernie. Sometimes, I think it would've been better if they'd got us all at the same time." She lapsed into silence again.

If it hadn't been for the almost unbearable pressure on his hand, Wayne would have panicked. She had stopped crying and she was so quiet that he might have imagined that she'd died. But, looking closely, the sheet on the bed rose and fell slightly.

In barely a whisper, she said, "The police gave us both a new identity. Dad was taken away from Ireland and I went into care in Belfast. Before Dad left, he made me promise not to contact anyone but I couldn't. . ." The heaving sobs

101

returned. "Bernie was a super friend – the best – and look what I did to her. I bet it was the IFG. And once they'd got the information out of her – that I was Cassie in Belfast – I guess it was only a matter of time before they traced me. The acid came from a Protestant crowd but that doesn't mean a Protestant threw it. I don't know. It'd be so easy for a bad guy to get in there."

Wayne was beginning to piece it all together. He'd heard about the IFG – the Irish Freedom Group – on the news. No wonder she needed a bodyguard and a panic alarm.

"If I'm right, it's only a matter of time before they catch up with me again."

Despite the sedatives, the grief exploded inside Cassie and only that hand kept her anchored to the real world.

SUGAR 16

Richard Clayton was elated by the result of Wayne's blood test. To combat a non-existent hypo, a police doctor had given Wayne the biggest slug of sugar he'd had since the nanorobots got to work in his body. Without insulin, the carbohydrate in his blood would have rocketed, making him thirsty, sick, fatigued. He would have been well on the road to acidosis and collapse. But the robots reacted brilliantly to the chemical shock, making and releasing insulin, keeping Wayne superbly on song and his body chemistry in balance.

He wasn't really diabetic any more. To avoid any further misunderstandings, Professor Clayton removed Wayne's tag with its out-of-date message about his medical condition. Now, Wayne was normal.

It was too soon to assess the effects of the other nanorobots on Wayne's general health but his heart had become more efficient and his physical condition had improved.

The counsellor looked ruefully at Cassie and said, "What *are* we going to do with you?"

"Nothing. I want to try again."

"Well, it's true we can't wrap you in cotton wool for ever. But going to a football match! You know you'll be uncomfortable in crowds – anything that reminds you of those clashes you had to put up with on the way to school."

"We weren't going to the match. We just got caught up in the crowd."

"That shows how careful you've got to be, Cassie. You've got to plan ahead. Stay indoors or arrange to be well away from Hillsborough for home matches. You've got to get Wayne sorted as well. He's got to help you organize."

Cassie was thinking, "Wayne? Organize?" But she didn't want to spend her time in hospital so she said, "Yes, he'll do that, no problem."

"And don't reckon on going to any music festivals."

"No, I won't. Promise."

"After all, Cassie, you've got something precious that you've got to protect."

"Yes, I know. My face." It was an important asset to herself and to the Department of Experimental Medicine.

The counsellor smiled. "That's Professor Staunton's game. No. Something much more important. I mean your mind."

"Miss Heywood?"

"Yes?"

"It's Professor Staunton here. With good news and bad."

At the other end of the line, Dorothy Heywood said, "Tell me, honey."

"Well, it's Face B – your favourite option."

"Forty years old, pretty as a picture."

"Yes," Hilary replied. "It's entirely compatible, I'm glad to say but. . ."

"What is it?"

"I have another client who's after it." Hilary didn't even notice that she'd used the word *client* rather than *patient*.

The singer seemed totally unperturbed. "That's all right, honey. Whatever she's offered, I'll double it. And if she raises her offer, I'll double *that*. If the deceased's family want more money or a donation to charity, I'll go along with anything. You see," Dorothy said with certainty, "I *will* have Face B."

In the body of the Irish bar, a woman was singing a raucous folk song, accompanied by two men on fiddles. One of the men was beating time energetically with his foot and whooping occasionally. In the corner, the three men huddled together over drinks were not listening to the music. They were well known in the pub and everyone kept a respectful distance. They were always served first at the bar and none of the other customers ever complained about the preferential treatment.

"The Brits have buried him so deep, it's not going to be easy to unearth him."

Unconcerned, the one in the baseball cap shrugged his huge shoulders. With a grin, he said, "But we've got his daughter."

"Have we?"

"As good as," Martin replied. "We've got a photograph of her going to school. Of course, she won't look like that any more. Not after . . . the acid." He smiled at a fond memory. "She'll stand out more now and we know which hospital they took her to."

"We also know she's been referred on but everyone's tight-lipped about it."

Martin adjusted his cap, leaned back in his chair and spread his arms. He was feeling good because it was his anniversary. On 15 August 1998, his organization – the Irish Freedom Group – had announced itself in spectacular style by killing 19 people with a car bomb in Newry. "She'll be somewhere in England. I've woken up every agent we've got and they're scouring around, particularly specialist units, looking for a girl – right age and physique – with a face full of scars. It's only a matter of time. And once we locate the traitor's daughter, we locate the traitor. He's bound to be visiting her now and again. For this one, we go all-out. No rest till we get him."

"So, we keep her under surveillance till he turns up?"

Martin shook his head and tutted. "No. He'd have tight security."

"What, then?"

"We take her. Then we trade. The traitor's daughter gets her freedom when we get the traitor." Martin smiled again and then added, "That's until we change our mind about her once we've got him."

There was a moment of silence and then a round of applause but it was for the musicians and not for the IFG members.

Hilary Staunton, Professor of Transplantation and Maxillofacial Surgery, was striding confidently into the theatre to carry out her fifth operation. Dorothy Heywood was about to cast off a dreadfully overworked face and thirty

106

years. The two women had a lot in common. They were both egotistical, vain and successful.

"OK," Hilary said to her team, "Let's get this show on the road. Cassie had twenty hours of microsurgery. The next one was the same even though I did some bone restoration as well. Then it was down to 18 hours. This one's straightforward. It's not a race – we're not doing it on a conveyor belt yet – but let's keep our concentration. Maximum efficiency's what I'm after." She cued the soothing music and began to remove Dorothy's eternally alarmed face.

17 PUS

By experimenting, Cassie and Wayne had worked out that it wasn't crowds alone that unnerved Cassie. She'd coped perfectly well with clubbing. It wasn't even crowds that shouted and took sides. She'd coped with a local league match and a tennis tournament that they'd stumbled upon in Hillsborough Park. It was the added ingredient of police control that made her flip. Swarming football fans and an anti-capitalist rally in the city centre had both pushed her to the edge of sanity.

Unlike Cassie, Wayne coped with things simply by not worrying about them.

Cassie had missed GCSEs because of her injuries. Wayne had missed them because he'd forgotten to turn up. Now, a year behind academically, they were required to try again. Wayne would not have bothered but, because Cassie was giving it a shot, he agreed to go along for the ride. Neither of them got on well with their home tutor, though. Wayne wasn't interested in algebra or the gender of French nouns or the Periodic Table or anything else and Cassie was too suspicious.

When the young teacher came into their house, he slipped one arm of his shades into the pocket of his long-sleeved shirt so the rest of his sunglasses overhung trendily. He must have been the only person in Sheffield not to have bare arms. He had ginger hair, alarmingly pale skin and, they guessed, a dislike of the sun. He smelled of sunscreen and his forehead, nose and ears were blotched pink with sunburn. When he introduced himself, Cassie listened carefully to his voice and asked, "Are you from Dublin?"

"Very good. Yes. And I guess you're from . . . I'm not sure . . . Donegal?"

Her dad had stressed how important it was to throw people off the scent, especially the ones who sounded friendly. "Close," she replied untruthfully. "Derry."

The tutor looked surprised – perhaps he was good at recognizing accents – but he began the lesson anyway.

Cassie kept turning her head so she could follow his every move. It was unlikely, she knew, that the bad guys would parachute in a teacher to sniff around but she was still wary of him.

There again, Cassie began to see threats everywhere. Even in the Hillsborough Co-op she drank her tea and whispered to Wayne, "There's a man on your left, four tables away, with a newspaper. See him? Well, I don't want to sound neurotic but I'm sure he's watching me."

Wayne glanced across. "He's reading the paper."

"Now, yes. But he *was* looking."

Wayne smiled. "I can think of a reason an old bloke would stare at you." She was wearing a tight T-shirt. With her bare arms and neck, she seemed to be saying to the world, "Look, I'm free of blemishes. I'm a normal girl." He hesitated, unsure of himself, and then added, "Like, if I was over there, I'd look at you."

Preoccupied, Cassie ignored the compliment. "I hope

he doesn't think I'm the girl in the car crash, the one whose face. . ." Full of summer cold, Cassie sneezed loudly.

"What was her name?" Wayne asked.

"I don't know. I got the impression I wouldn't have been told so I didn't bother asking. Maybe they didn't want me to try and trace her. Maybe they frown on morbid curiosity. Anyway, I don't think I want to know. It's too personal."

"You're not really like her. You're . . . in between."

"He's put his paper down and he's. . ."

"Maybe he's wondering why *you're* looking at *him*."

"I'm worried in case. . ." She shook her head and picked up her cup. "Never mind. Let's drink up and get going."

"Yeah," Wayne said, keen to play the part of secret agent. "That way, we'll see if he tails us."

He didn't. Or, as Cassie was thinking, he was brilliant at following people discreetly.

In a quiet period, Hilary was typing the introduction to her research paper. It took her mind off the latest operation. Dorothy Heywood's face transplant had thrown up some unexpected complications. It had taken a gruelling 24 hours of surgery and Hilary still had her reservations about the outcome. Of course, those reservations would not appear in her article.

Human beings have an intricate immune system to disarm and reject viruses, bacteria and other foreign tissue that invades the body. Unfortunately unable to distinguish disease-carrying germs from the foreign cells of a vital transplant, the immune system attacks both.

Currently, this immune reaction is the largest hurdle to transplanting organs and tissues (along with a shortage of donated material).

Transplantation involves the transfer of tissue or an organ (a) from one human being to another or (b) from one part of the body to another. As rejection is not an issue in scenario (b), this paper deals solely with transplants from a donor to a recipient (a). Traditionally, these transplants have been carried out for life-saving purposes and require careful matching of donor and recipient as well as a cocktail of immunosuppressive drugs.

Transplant technology was pioneered in 1905 when sight was restored to damaged eyes by transplanting corneas. The first internal organs to be transplanted successfully were kidneys in the 1950s. Now, mainstream transplant procedures are available for hearts, liver, pancreatic tissue, lungs, bone and bone marrow. Most transplant material is taken from deceased donors but, less commonly, a kidney or part of a liver may be taken from living donors.

Advances in tolerance therapy and microsurgery reported herein allow transplant methodology to expand confidently from life-saving techniques to reconstructive surgery.

A nurse put his head round the door and said, "I think you should take a look at Dorothy Heywood."

Hilary saved the document, shut down the laptop and hurried to her patient in one of the private rooms.

As soon as the surgeon entered, Dorothy complained in a pathetic voice that was very difficult to decipher, "It's hurting, honey."

Hilary bent over her and said comfortingly, "You've got severe bruising, as you'd expect, stitches and dressings. It's not a surprise that it's feeling tender. Unfortunately, it's not going to go away at the drop of a hat. I'll top up your painkillers, though." Inside, Hilary was in a panic. Dorothy Heywood's forty-year-old face was too discoloured in some places and far too pale in others. Here and there, the outer layer of skin was flaking off. The swelling around the incision was not reducing as quickly as it had with her other patients. Alarmingly, there were the first signs of a lesion near her left eye and the skin was cold to the touch. Either the transplant tissue was not getting a good supply of blood so it was deprived of oxygen and food, or the anti-rejection medicine was not working so her white blood cells had begun to wage war on the young tissue. Either way, the face could be dying.

Hilary had convinced herself that necrosis just couldn't happen. She was too good a surgeon and her drug was too good at suppressing the immune reaction to suffer a catastrophic breakdown. During the operation, she'd found it tricky to reconnect the elderly nerves and blood vessels but she'd done it. Brilliantly. It could be that, in Dorothy, the internal healing was so slow that some cells were dying before the joined branches of the carotid artery could support a healthy blood supply to the face and the repaired jugular vein could carry away waste. Hilary could only hope that the blood vessels would recover in time to bring back life-giving blood before too much of the transplant was destroyed. Then, if they did, Dorothy's own body would mend any damage just as it repaired any normal cut or bruise and the singer would get her new improved appearance after a longer recuperation period.

To Hilary, it was inconceivable that Dorothy Heywood and her new face could part company. It would be a disaster for her burgeoning research.

But Professor Staunton changed her mind two days later. The singer's rapid deterioration left Hilary in no doubt that she had a major problem on her hands. Within days, Dorothy's face was swollen, blistered and discoloured. It was a darker shade from the surrounding skin as if it had come from a donor of a different ethnic group. Deep lesions and the foul smell of decaying flesh announced the death of the transplant tissue. Some of the wounds leaked yellow pus, full of infection. Each time Hilary pumped another antibiotic into her failing patient, the bacteria weakened and then came back with a vengeance to colonize the face afresh.

If the transplant had been a hand or an arm, Hilary would have amputated it by now to stop the bacteria's poison spreading and killing the patient. After all, a hand transplant could always be tried again with a different donor. But a face! She couldn't amputate a face, keep the patient alive until a new donor came along, and try again. No one could withstand that degree of shock.

Dorothy was beyond uttering words but her erratic hand movements over her stomach told Hilary that she had abdominal pain. Even without eating, Dorothy vomited green fluids copiously. Drenched with sweat, she had a high fever and her heartbeat was soaring. Diarrhoea was making her lose weight dramatically. The facial skin around the oval incision had died and ruptured, revealing lifeless muscle underneath. Even though the room had air-conditioning, the stench had become unbearable and no amount of fragrance could overpower it for long.

Hilary worked around the clock, testing Dorothy's tissue, the oozing liquids, everything she could think of. She also tried every treatment that might have a beneficial effect while her patient was dosed to the eyeballs with morphine. It was the analysis of Dorothy's body fluids that finally nailed the problem. It wasn't that Dorothy was too old to heal quickly enough. Rather, her body was too good at recognizing the anti-rejection drug as a foreign substance and ejecting it. Hilary detected high concentrations of the immunosuppressant in every fluid that flowed from her. It meant there wasn't enough drug circulating inside her to dampen her immune system. Free to function, Dorothy's white blood cells were blindly and effectively loosening her tenuous hold on the transplanted face.

After a massive injection of a cocktail of different anti-rejection drugs, Dorothy had a day of respite before her stubborn immune system kicked in again. It seemed that nothing could persuade her body chemistry to cease hostilities against the face.

Hilary Staunton had explored every angle and there was nothing left in her arsenal. Helpless, she sat with her head in her hands. It was only a matter of time before she lost her patient.

The kiss seemed more real this time. Finally feeling that they were *her* lips, Cassie experienced it first-hand. It was awkward, embarrassing, completely lacking in passion, and all over in a couple of seconds. When actors kissed in films, it was always proficient, prolonged and deeply romantic. It wasn't like that in real life. Cassie wasn't even sure why she had allowed Wayne to kiss her. She guessed that she wanted to prove to herself that she was attractive to the opposite sex. Besides, Wayne wasn't that bad. He had his good points. And he was there, available. But he wasn't a good kisser. That was something else she'd have to teach him, like how to use a washing machine and clean the toilet.

But Cassie was uncertain for another reason. She was wondering who Wayne had fallen for. Was it the anonymous girl whose face Cassie was wearing, the old Cassie, the new Cassie? She barely knew who she was herself.

"I've been meaning to ask," Wayne muttered. "Is it . . . you know . . . all you from the neck downwards?"

Cassie hesitated, expecting a sneeze that didn't come, and then coughed instead. "What are you trying to say, Wayne? Spit it out."

"I just wondered if you'd had to have . . . like . . . other transplants."

One hesitant and clumsy kiss and her flatmate thought he was entitled to get personal. Teasing him, Cassie said, "Ah, you mean my hands. They were fixed with normal skin grafts."

"No, I mean. . ."

"What?"

"You know." He glanced down at her body.

Cassie decided it was too painful to watch him struggling, not daring to ask a direct question about her breasts. To put him out of his misery, she said, "My clothes protected most of me. It's all me."

Wayne let out a sigh of relief and then hesitated. "Not that . . . you know. It wouldn't turn me off if. . ." Even more tongue-tied, he added, "I were just hoping you'd not been hurt more than. . . It weren't as if I meant your. . ." He glanced down at her chest.

"You're in a hole, Wayne, so I'd stop digging if I were you."

Wayne nodded. "It's just that you're a right good shape. I'm glad it's all you."

Cassie was beginning to think she'd have to train Wayne in everything but, as far as diplomacy was concerned, she'd probably be wasting her time. "Let's cool it," she said. "We've got a house to clean."

Wayne groaned.

"Have you seen the state of the toilet? Being a boy, I don't suppose you notice such things." With her bouts of diarrhoea, she had no choice but to notice and to clean it regularly. Trying to make light of the unpleasantness, she said, "We might as well have it nice because I read somewhere the average person spends three years of their life on the loo."

For once, Wayne was fast with his response. "On it or quite close to it," he said with a wide smile.

116

"Yes. Sometimes not quite close enough in your case, I've noticed."

Wayne shrugged happily.

The frenzy of cleaning was almost as short-lived as the kiss. They'd both forgotten that they were due a visit from their tutor. It was going to be a special session. He had got permission from the headteacher to take them to their school so they could look around and familiarize themselves with the place in the peace and quiet of the summer vacation.

Halfway to the school, a blue Astra pulled up by the three of them and a male head in a baseball cap leaned out of the driver's window. "Excuse me. Do you know where. . .?"

Cassie took fright at the Irish accent. It was just too much of a coincidence. She was about to run down the road when the tutor grabbed her and bundled her, kicking and screaming into the back of the car.

Wayne cried, "Hey! You can't. . ."

He didn't get any further. Another man appeared from nowhere, cracked him on the back of his head and dragged his limp body into a second car.

The kidnap was complete in a matter of seconds. With screeching tyres, the bad guys took off with their priceless pawn.

18 PETROL

The whole ordeal would have been bearable if he'd still been with Cassie but, when Wayne came to, she was nowhere to be seen. He was sitting on the hard wooden floor of a gloomy garden shed and the only other people in there were two bad guys. The only light was a little sunshine that penetrated the cracks in the slatted walls. Ominously, Wayne's hands were tied to a post behind his back and all sorts of tools – shears, a rake, a spade – were dangling from hooks. In one corner, there was a petrol-driven lawn mower.

The first man – sitting in a green plastic chair – leaned forward and said in an Irish accent, "Welcome, Wayne W Wingate." He sniggered and added, "Quite a mouthful."

The second bad guy was the ginger-haired tutor and he was standing silently behind the first. If he had been in range, Wayne would have spat at him.

"This Cassie O'Rourke. Who is she?"

"Fuck off."

The bad guy with the broad shoulders and cap laughed aloud. "Another mouthful." He sat back, fiddling with the secateurs in his hands. "I'm in no rush. I just want to know about your Cassie." He bent down and dragged forward a plastic petrol can. Presumably, its contents were used to fuel the mower. He left it at his feet, smiled and looked back at his captive. "You live with her," he stated. "That means you'll know all her little secrets. Who is she?"

"She's Cassie," Wayne answered with a gulp. "That's it."

"Where's she from?"

"I don't know. Ireland."

"*Northern* Ireland?"

"Suppose."

The bad guy dropped the secateurs, reached down for the plastic can, lifted it up on to his lap and, taking his time, unscrewed the cap. He bent over it, breathed in deeply through his nose and grimaced. He weighed the can theatrically in his hand and muttered, "Plenty left." Then he stood up, fitted the pourer and tipped it up so a dribble of fuel ran on to the floorboards and Wayne's trainers. Some of the liquid soaked chillingly into Wayne's socks. "Where did you say she was from?"

"Northern Ireland."

"Where exactly?"

"Dunno."

"You don't live with someone without finding out a lot about them."

Wayne was quaking, hoping that he wasn't going to wet himself. "She . . . er . . . didn't say much about her past."

"What about her present?"

Wayne shrugged.

"We know she's missed a lot of school because she's been ill. What was the problem?"

"Dunno. Didn't like to talk about it," Wayne said.

The man laughed again. "Life with you two must have been a riot! You never even spoke."

This time, the petrol dripped into Wayne's jeans.

"Let's put it this way. Has she had her face fixed recently?"

"Her face?"

"You know, the thing you speak out of. Except, I was forgetting, you never say anything. Tell you what, Wayne Wingate. Break a habit of a lifetime. Tell me about her."

Wayne remembered Cassie's hysterical rant. He could almost hear her tormented voice saying, "They poured petrol over her. They tortured the information out of her. And when they got it, they set fire to her anyway." Wayne shuddered. Like Bernie, he wasn't brave. He was scared stiff. But he knew something that Bernie never knew. If they were going to burn him, no matter what he said, he might as well say nothing or lie. "Fuck off," he said again.

The man made a tutting noise with his tongue. "Such language. I was hoping for a more . . . friendly attitude. With language like that, I bet Cassie hardly dared introduce you to her mum and dad."

"She. . ." Wayne stopped himself. He was determined not to help them identify Cassie as the Cassie they wanted so he stopped himself saying that she didn't have a mother.

"Yes? Go on."

"Fuck off."

The shed was hot and airless. The petrol fumes were giving Wayne a headache. If the bad guys lit a match now, the whole place would go up in flames.

"It's amazing what they can do with surgery these days, isn't it?"

"Dunno."

"No, medicine's not my strong point either. I'm better at putting people in hospital than sending them home, fit and well. I do wonder, though, if doctors can build a whole new face. What do you think?"

Wayne did his best to look baffled. "No idea."

The bad guy squatted next to Wayne and prodded his cheek. "I had a good look at you. Can't see any scars. Have you had a new face, Wayne Wingate?"

"No."

"Do you want one?" he snapped, his voice harsh for the first time.

Wayne found it difficult to swallow. "No."

"Why's there a panic button in your house?"

It took Wayne several seconds to fish around for an answer. "It's for me."

"Oh?"

"I'm diabetic, me, and I get highs and lows."

"So, it's a hotline to the hospital?"

"Yes."

"Not to the police?"

"No."

The man shook his head as if admonishing Wayne. "I don't believe you." He stood up again and, with glee, poured petrol over Wayne's head.

Wayne couldn't even scream or swear without breathing in the horrible liquid. He cringed, closed his eyes and mouth, and blew air from his nose to keep it away.

"I think we've established that neither of us is any good at medicine, but what about chemistry?"

Wayne couldn't open his smarting eyes. "Chemistry?"

"What do you know about sulphuric acid?"

"Nothing," he struggled to say through pursed lips.

Unseen, the voice came close to his ear. "You know nothing but you've told me all I want."

"What?" He spat the drips of fuel from his mouth.

"Think about it. If you really didn't know Cassie's past, all this would make no sense to you at all. You'd be screaming, 'Why do you want to know about her? What's sulphuric acid got to do with it? What are you talking about? Why are you doing this?' No. Nice try, Wayne, but you're not puzzled enough."

"But I *don't* know what you're talking—"

The bad guy interrupted him. "Too late."

For once in his life, Wayne had been so careful in everything he'd said because he knew it would be easy to betray his girlfriend through his words. He was gutted to realize his silence had betrayed her instead. In a daze, he heard two sets of footsteps move away and out of the shed. Utterly petrified and devastated, his tears mixing with the petrol, he held his breath, waiting for the fire to catch.

Alone in the shabby bedroom, gagged, her wrists tied painfully tightly to the headboard, Cassie was out of her mind with fear. There were two reasons. These were the bad guys who created incalculable havoc with their explosives, nails, fire and, of course, their acid. Whenever their footprints touched a place, nothing was left untainted. She was frightened also because they'd searched her bag and taken away her few remaining green pills.

Without anti-rejection pills, without an effective means of closing down her ruthless immune system, Dorothy Heywood didn't stand a chance. A week after the operation, her face turned black and fell apart. The infection multiplied like wildfire, spreading its poison into every vital organ. The woman who wanted only to look attractive died in the ugliest possible fashion.

Of course, the contract that Dorothy had signed acknowledged an element of risk. Professor Staunton could do her best and no more. Should there be unforeseen complications, the surgeon could be blamed only if it could be proved that she had been negligent or incompetent. Hilary had tried her utmost and her previous successful operations were a testament to her competence. In law, she was in the clear. But her sponsors might see things differently. They would gladly empty their purses and wallets if they had to risk a scar or two to regain their youthful appearance but risking death was a different matter. It was crucial to Hilary to make sure that everyone knew Dorothy Heywood was an isolated case, a one-in-a-million accident and a victim of her own unique body chemistry.

Luckily, the Department of Experimental Medicine enjoyed a close relationship with the local coroner. Hilary picked up the phone and invited him to a business lunch where they could discuss matters of mutual interest.

19 PETALS

When Cassie heard the sound of shoes on the stairs, she screamed inwardly. Outwardly, she couldn't make a sound. The man who'd pulled up in the blue car and begun to ask her for directions came into the bedroom, followed by the treacherous tutor.

"Welcome," the first man said with mock cheerfulness. "We've just been having a chat with your boyfriend." His accent, like the tutor's, was thick Dublin. He nodded to the tutor who walked up to Cassie and removed the gag.

If her mouth hadn't been so dry, she would have spat at him.

"He spilled the beans, Cassie. Good choice of name, by the way. I like Cassie. How's your dad?"

Cassie was well aware that Wayne was short on judgment and thoughtfulness. She hadn't known him for long enough to measure his loyalty or courage. But even though Bernie's loyalty and courage had been endless, she'd still talked under the Irish Freedom Group's brutality. "What have you done to him?"

"Ah. Isn't that touching? Not, 'What are you going to do to me?' but, 'What have you done to him?' Young love's a wonderful thing." The man walked towards her and studied her face just like that old singer had done. The peak of his baseball cap touched her hair, making her wince. His coarse finger followed her faint scar and then lingered threateningly under her chin. "You can hardly see the join. Nice work. Very pretty. You're like a flower with new petals." He shook his head. "Amazing the lengths people go to when they don't want to be recognized. You had us fooled for a while – till your teacher heard rumours about swapping faces. And we were thinking we'd marked you for life. This time, it'll have to be more . . . permanent."

Cassie shivered because it felt as if a large insect was crawling around her skin, but she couldn't swat it away. She tried to stay focused, tried to keep the panic at bay. "Have you killed him?" she stammered.

"My name's Martin, by the way. I don't see why we can't be on first name terms for our time together. I'm an ex-colleague of your dad – the traitor."

"Have you killed Wayne?"

"Yes."

Cassie's head slumped to one side. Her mother, her brothers, Bernie and now Wayne. Once the bad guys killed her, the whole business would come to an end with the murder of her dad. Maybe then this Martin would be satisfied. Except that, by then, he'd be addicted to cruelty so he'd have to find an excuse to persecute some other family. She sniffed, tried to gather some strength. "How are you going to kill me?"

"I like that as well," Martin replied. "Dignity and bottle. No pleading, no blubbing. Not like that girlfriend of yours, Bernadette. And far more upfront than your two-faced father."

Cassie had her fair share of blubbing to do but she refused to do it in front of these monsters. "How?"

Really enjoying himself, he shrugged nonchalantly. "For you, flower, I'll do it quickly," Martin promised, as if he were doing her a favour. "But it won't be for a while. Days or even weeks. Who knows? It depends on the traitor."

Cassie nodded. "You're using me to lure him here."

"Dignity, bottle and intelligence," Martin said. "You didn't get that from your father. It'll be a pity to kill you."

Cassie was finding it hard to breathe in the presence of this grotesque bully. "You won't."

"Oh?"

"You won't get Dad either. Not like that."

"And why not?"

She paused to fight the welling tears. "This face might look good now but I'm rejecting it. It's called an immune reaction. I'll be dead in a few days." She didn't know what sort of death she'd have to endure if she lost her face but she had already resolved not to mention her anti-rejection pills. She thought she'd rather die slowly by her own immune system than quickly at the hands of terrorists.

Martin spread out his arms in a gesture of surrender. "I'm easily bamboozled by medicine. I concede to your superior knowledge." He walked up to her bedside, knelt down and whispered, "But, let me tell you, I'm not so easily bamboozled by people. Nice try, but I don't believe it. You're bluffing. And, even if it's true, your dad will come anyway – if only to check if you're really dead. People are so sentimental like that."

Cassie was consumed with trying to hold herself together. She realized that Martin liked playing games with people but it hadn't dawned on her straightaway that he had already toyed with her. Trying to control her descent into anxiety, she saw hope for Wayne. She uttered, "You haven't killed Wayne, have you? You need him as an intermediary."

"You can't have enough dignity and bottle but you can overdo the intelligence. People who are too clever get on my nerves after a bit. Remember, I can lure your dad here whether you're alive or not."

Cassie came back a little from the brink. She'd had her triumph. She was sure now that Wayne was alive. But she was still tied to a bed, completely at the mercy of heartless terrorists and, without her medication, she had already started to die.

Wayne had spent a long time listening. There wasn't much else he could do while he was gagged and bound in the darkened shed. He couldn't reach the shears or secateurs to cut himself free. He was helpless. And he felt ill. It wasn't a high or a low; they were things of the past. He just felt drained. Perhaps it was the effect of being imprisoned in a garden shed for hours. Perhaps it was the lingering effect of the petrol fumes. Perhaps it was the mental strain. Apart from that time he'd passed out in a police cell, he'd never thought about his own mortality. The frailty of life was something old people had to worry about, not him. But when he heard footsteps on the gravel outside, all of his fear returned.

The door swung open and the colourless tutor in sunglasses stepped out of the dazzling sunlight. He was on his own this time. He didn't waste words. He merely announced, "You're free to go." He took away the bandage that cut across Wayne's mouth.

"What?" Wayne imagined this was going to be a very sick joke.

"You're out of here."

Still wary, Wayne muttered, "Oh?"

"Just one condition. I'm going to blindfold you and drive you back into Hillsborough. Then you go home and press that panic button – the one that'll bring in the cops. Yes," he added, "I did know about it. Social Services told me so I knew you were lying. Anyway, you give your friends a little message. Nice and simple. Can you manage that?"

Wayne stared at him with open hostility.

"You tell them we've got Cassie. We hand her over once we get the traitor. No wires, no cops or snipers, no phones, no weapons, no tricks, nothing. Just the traitor on his own. Once he agrees to that, you'll set up the time and a place."

"Me? What time and place?"

The tutor smiled. "We're not going to tell you that now, are we? They'd set a trap. You'll get to know when we want you to know. We'll call."

Wayne began to believe that he really was about to be released – because the terrorists had a use for him. "What makes you think I'll do it?"

"You'll cooperate because I've seen how you look at her, like a little girl looking at a puppy. You want her back, don't you?"

Wayne didn't have to respond. The blindfold on, the rope around his wrists cut away, he was guided to a car and, thirty minutes later, he was wandering in a daze down a backstreet in Hillsborough. It was all so bewildering, so sudden, as if he'd just walked out of a cinema after seeing an involving thriller. Only this time, the story spilled over dangerously into reality.

Wayne had always coped with all the shit that life threw at him by walking away. Right now, there was even more reason to walk away. The hospital had fixed his diabetes and things had got really heavy around Cassie. When mad terrorists threatened to set him on fire, when they told him to deal with the feds, it was time not just to walk away but to run like crazy. Besides, it wasn't his problem. Let Cassie, her dad, the bad guys and the feds sort it out between themselves. Nothing to do with him.

There again, he'd sworn to be Cassie's friend. More than a friend. And Cassie needed two things: she needed to escape and she needed a fresh supply of her green pills. He knew she was due at the hospital soon for a check-up and to collect her next batch of tablets. Besides, Wayne had a good idea where he'd been held. Perhaps that meant he also knew where the bad guys were keeping Cassie. He couldn't walk away with that knowledge.

While he waited for the police to come, Wayne had plenty of time to think. Sure, he was out of his depth. Sure, he should tell them that he thought he knew roughly where the bad guys were hanging out. But every instinct told him to keep it to himself. Over the years, he'd found out for himself what feds were like. They weren't his friends. They weren't to be trusted. It was like the arrest down the road. Just one word – ecstasy – and they'd jump in with both feet and come to the wrong conclusion. He didn't want heavy-handed feds barging in on the terrorists, forcing them to take their revenge on Cassie. Out of his depth or not, he'd much rather try to rescue her himself. At least he could trust himself.

It was a funny couple of feds who arrived. No uniforms and they treated Wayne like a human being, like he was important. The chief one had an annoying habit of sniffing a lot. Together, they asked a hundred questions about his kidnap and showed him a hundred photos of dodgy-looking blokes. The tutor was easy to identify, of course, and Wayne thought the leader was a man listed simply as Martin. The feds nodded encouragingly at Wayne and glanced significantly at each other but didn't make any comments about the men he'd identified.

When the police had finished with him, they gave him a free mobile phone – a secure one, the first he'd ever owned legitimately – and a secret number to report any developments. On their way out, the one who kept sniffing said, "Thanks. We'll talk to Cassie's dad, work out how we're going to play this, and get back to you."

As soon as they were out of sight, Wayne headed for the tram and the hospital. He went through his usual check-up with a nurse and did not raise the topic of Cassie O'Rourke. It was easy to avoid talking about her because Professor Clayton and his staff were into diabetes and nanorobots. They didn't have time to worry about someone else's speciality as well. Also, he didn't mention that he felt edgy and rough. Under the circumstances, it was hardly surprising. It probably had nothing to do with his old illness or his hi-tech treatment.

When the nurse had taken all of the readings she needed,

Wayne made to leave. But when he thought no one was watching – except a couple of senile patients who were on a different planet altogether – he put another secret number to use. He slipped into a side-room in the hope of finding a face-transplant case and those little green pills. He aimed to snatch a good quantity because Cassie needed them. No doubt the department would simply replace any lost ones so Cassie wouldn't have to worry about depriving another patient.

There was someone in the bed but Wayne couldn't see who it was because a sheet was pulled right up, covering the patient entirely. There was no sign of movement at all under the eerie sheet. Two other things struck him. The air-conditioning in the room made it really cold and the smell was awful.

Wayne tiptoed forward, trying not to wake the patient. On the bedside cabinet, there were three plastic containers and the second one he opened contained pills that looked exactly like Cassie's green immunosuppressants. He put them in his pocket but then decided to make absolutely sure he'd got the right ones. All he had to do was to risk taking a look at the patient. If there were signs of a transplant, he'd know the pills were the same as Cassie's.

He took hold of the white sheet and very slowly pulled it back. The colour in his face drained away completely when he saw a woman with a partly shaven head. Between clumps of her remaining hair, dyed jet-black, there was hardly a face at all. It was just a pulverized mass of gashes. It could have been a gorilla's face that had been pummelled and cut to ribbons. Wayne didn't want to look at the vile thing but he couldn't tear his eyes away. The flesh had fallen back from her yellowed teeth and underneath the festering skin there was a clear view of diseased sinew and bone.

He didn't know he was looking at a woman whose glamorous features had once decorated the sleeve of a record but he did know now the fate that awaited Cassie. He turned away, threw up all over the floor and then stumbled out of the room. Hardly in control of his legs, he dashed out of the ward. Behind him, he heard raised voices. "Hey! What do you think you're doing?" "Wayne, is that you?" "Come back here!" He ignored them all.

STEEL 20

Wayne was sitting on the ground in Knoll Top, just up Nanny Hill, with his hands feeling the earth beside him. Down below in the valley was Stocksbridge steel works. The hill opposite was Green Moor with its dotted farmhouses, woodland and pylons. He breathed in deeply, still trying to rid himself of that appalling smell of decay.

There it was again. A distinctive earth-trembling thump. It came from the steel works and he was sure it was the noise he'd heard in that garden shed. It sounded exactly right: the right volume and tone, the right judder, the right echo. He knew the sound because he used to hear it sometimes when he was younger and he went to the big sports centre along Manchester Road. Now, all he had to do was to find a house that had been bought or rented recently by Irish tenants. He was guessing that he'd been kept in the garden shed while Cassie was in the house itself. Of course, the bad guys could have taken her to London or Scotland or Australia or anywhere but he could follow only his one lead and he guessed they'd stay in or near Sheffield.

Stocksbridge wasn't a big place but, even so, finding the house with a garden shed would be almost impossible. He knew it wouldn't be isolated because he'd been gagged. There must have been other houses within earshot. But he couldn't lie in wait at every house with a shed, hoping to spot mad Irishmen coming and going. There was a chance of finding them, though. He went in search of Felix.

The boy who used to go swimming with him years ago wasn't at home. He was hanging out with friends at Stubbin shops. He was a lot bigger than he used to be and almost all of his hair had been shaved off. Sitting in the doorway of a shuttered and dilapidated shop, his face creased up. "Wayne? Is that you? Hey. What brings you here?"

"You."

"Me? Oh, no. You're not still on the scrounge, are you? Things don't change much."

"You know your dad?" Wayne asked.

"Yes, I think so. He's the chap I see every day, isn't he?"

"Is he still a postman?"

Felix frowned, wondering what was coming next. "Yes."

"I remember, he always used to boast he knew everyone in Stocksbridge."

"You don't want to believe that, but he's hot on his own patch. He knows everyone's birthday, who's got divorced, who gets dirty magazines, where their bills come from, all that sort of stuff. He reckons he can suss everyone out just by seeing their post. He sees and hears things on his round as well." Felix shrugged. "So what?"

"I've got to, like, have a quick chat with him."

"Oh? Why?"

Wayne should have expected this question but he hadn't thought it through. "Well . . . er. . . It's important."

"Yeah?"

"I'm looking for some Irish guys who've just moved here."

"Why?"

"Er . . . there's this girl living with them. . ."

Felix interrupted enthusiastically. "You met her at a party and, in a drunken stupor, you lost the piece of paper she gave you with her address and number."

"Yeah, that's it."

"She must be pretty good to drag you out here on a wild goose chase."

"Suppose."

"OK. I'd better go back for tea anyway or Mum'll kill me – again. Come on."

Wayne knew it was unlikely that the bad guys would have had any mail. That would've risked their security, he imagined. But a postman would know if someone new had just moved into an empty house. Someone who didn't get any post would probably stand out as unusual. Maybe the postman had seen an unfamiliar car, like a blue Astra. The bad guys would probably have ditched it by now – left it burned out on derelict ground somewhere – but there was no harm in trying.

Felix's father was happy to help. He was proud of his power to deduce everyone's lifestyle from their letters. He knew who was into motor racing, who bought their clothes from catalogues, who was in which unions, who had a home computer. But he didn't have any recent changes on his patch. Seeing Wayne's expression of disappointment, though, he volunteered to check it out with his five colleagues who covered the rest of Stocksbridge. "Or you could ask them yourself. You'd just have to come to the Victoria Street depot at five tomorrow."

"Five? In the morning?"

"Ah, I forgot. You teenagers don't think anything happens before school time, do you? Time doesn't exist before eight-thirty."

Instead, Wayne agreed to catch up with him on his Stubbin round at nine-thirty.

That night, Wayne took a phone call from an angry Martin who complained that Wayne had been out too much. In his third attempt to make contact, Martin ordered Wayne to stay at home to take messages about Cassie and to pass information back from her dad.

"Well," Wayne replied, "I've got a mobile now. You can use that."

"Ah. The Anti-Terror Squad's been it's usual generous self. OK. And tell me what they said."

Wayne dictated the number and then brought him up to date, not that there was much to report.

"I bet they got you to identify me, yes?"

Wayne hesitated.

"You don't have to be shy. They'll have shown you an identity parade of mugshots."

"You're Martin."

At the other end of the line, the man laughed, recovering that unnerving sense of humour. "The police invent codenames for operations, Cassie's an alias, her father never gave us his real name. It's amazing how many people are using names their mothers' wouldn't recognize. Martin will do, though. Wayne W Wingate sounds false as well."

"It's not."

"All right, W-W-W dot. We'll phone you around midday and in the evening every day. Understand? If you want

Cassie back, the calls take priority over everything else."

"You could just give me your number."

Cynically, Martin retorted, "Would you like our full names, addresses, hand swabs and fingerprints as well?"

"Dunno. Your number will do."

"Yeah, and within minutes I'll have the cops at the door. Don't be naïve." He put the phone down.

Wayne shrugged. When he dialled 1471, he found that he'd just been called by a withheld number. He sat down in front of the television on his own. It was his telly and he could watch whatever he wanted, untroubled by anyone else. He'd never had it so good. Absolute heaven. But somehow, it fell flat. Flicking through the channels, he couldn't get interested in any of the programmes. He was preoccupied with tomorrow's possibilities.

Wayne caught up with Felix's dad as he stood by someone's gate swearing loudly at a Yorkshire Terrier that was running up and down the lawn and yapping ridiculously.

"Not going in there," he muttered darkly. "Not till the dog's away."

"You could just step on it," Wayne said. "That'd shut it up."

"The company won't let me. I can only kick it if it's got its teeth in my leg. It's a bit late, then." While he waited for the owner to catch her agitated dog, he gave Wayne three addresses in Stocksbridge. "All of them's got new people in but no one's seen a girl your age."

Wayne wrote the addresses in biro on his left palm and said, "Thanks. That's great. I'll take it from here."

The dog had been locked indoors so the postman opened the gate. From the path, he said, "Good luck. Hope you find her."

"Cheers." Immediately, Wayne headed for the first house. It was in Kenworthy Road, just along from the high school. Knowing that it would be a disaster if he were spotted by the bad guys, he stayed well back while still trying to get a good look at the semi-detached house. Almost at once, Wayne dismissed it from his list of possibilities. At the side, a new garage was being attached. He doubted very much if terrorists would extend a house while they occupied it. Besides, as a captive, Wayne had spent a good few hours listening and he hadn't heard anything that sounded like a building site. There was no sign of a blue Astra, either.

The second possibility was a small stone-built cottage on Hollin Busk Lane but Wayne couldn't get near the front of it without being seen. He decided instead to creep through the long grass of the farmland at the back of the rural bungalow. Carefully peering over a low dry-stone wall at the bottom of the garden, he saw paving slabs leading from the back door to the shed. His heart sank. The hut looked bigger and more solid than the one in which he'd been kept. And four other things bothered him. He was in a field with sheep and, in the next one, there were cows. Further down the hill, he could see horses. Yet, when he'd been imprisoned, he hadn't heard any farm animals. In the air was that unpleasant farmyard smell with a faint additional whiff from the fish and chip shop round the corner. Wayne hadn't smelled anything like that. And he definitely remembered the sound of approaching footsteps on gravel.

When he'd been led out of the shed, he'd felt small stones underneath his trainers. The atmosphere was all wrong. He was a long way up from the steel works, virtually in the countryside, and he doubted if anyone could hear industrial noise from here.

For years, Wayne had hated cats, just like the postman with his phobia for dogs. Wayne stood up and shooed away the ginger tom that was wondering whether to rub against the stranger's legs in the hope of getting attention or food. Wayne picked up a handful of soil and threw it hard at the cat and then walked away, back down the hill towards the centre of the village.

His last address was quite close to the sports centre and the steel works. Knowing that this was likely to be the one where the bad guys were hiding out, Wayne inched cautiously along the tiny Albany Road. His heartbeat leaped when he saw a blue Astra parked in front of the house. Getting closer, he also noticed a gravel path at the end of the terrace. Feeling vulnerable, he drew in a sharp breath and speeded up, walking briskly past the house and round the corner so he could see into the rear garden. He was not sure if he was relieved or disheartened to see that the house didn't have a shed. He felt helpless. For one reason or another, he'd just written off the only leads he had.

Walking down the footpath towards Manchester Road to get a bus back to Hillsborough, he had an idea. The cogs in Wayne's brain had always turned at a leisurely pace. He abandoned any thought of a bus home and went back to the house in Kenworthy Road instead.

Sneaking silently down the drive, avoiding the scaffolding

and piles of bricks, he hid behind the half-built garage and peeked into the garden. The small area of untidy lawn was split by a gravel path leading to a shabby garden shed. Behind it, there was a fence and the school's deserted playing field. Suddenly aware that he was in great danger, Wayne sank down behind the incomplete brickwork and squatted on the ground, making himself as small as possible. Knowing it was crucial not to be seen or heard, he tried to make sure he was not visible from any of the windows. It was then that his mobile decided to play a tune.

Unfamiliar with the phone, he took a few seconds of fiddling to answer the call. "Yes?" he whispered.

It was a man with an English accent and he assumed that Wayne knew who he was. "Where are you? In the open by the sound of it."

"Yes. Er . . . in a playing field."

"Can you talk?"

"Suppose."

"You don't have to whisper, do you?" The security officer sniffed loudly.

Now, Wayne could picture who he was talking to: the chief with the snuffle. "There's people quite near."

"OK. Just listen. We've talked to Cassie's father and he's prepared to meet them. Got that?"

"Yes."

"But he needs evidence Cassie's alive and OK before he shows."

"Right," said Wayne. He was crouching even lower now, like a frightened rabbit, not knowing whether to stay still or make a run for it. He looked around wildly, hoping that the bad guys hadn't heard the phone and come out to discover him.

"We think it's best if you demand to see her and report back, but you'll have to negotiate that – or come to some other arrangement. OK?"

"Got it."

"Right. Call us with any developments."

Still speaking in a hushed voice, Wayne said, "Before you ring off, you know that Martin?"

"Yes?"

"What is he?"

"What do you mean? He's a prominent member of the IFG."

"But what does he do? What's his job?"

"He's a builder."

"A builder."

"Yes. Why?"

"Er. . . Nothing. I were just wondering." Now Wayne was sure. The bad guy was posing as a builder. The reason there were no noises from the garage while Wayne was tied in the shed was because Martin was too busy terrorizing his captives.

"He's also a weight-lifter and a nifty boxer. Not a man to meet on a dark night. That tutor of yours is an expert bomb-maker and Martin is a fearless handler of explosives. Quite a combination, not to be messed with."

Sitting right outside their house, Wayne gulped.

21 BRICK

It was easy to imagine what it was like to stake out a house and rescue someone inside when the opportunity arose – after all, Wayne had seen all the right films – but it seemed ridiculously tough when he was huddled inside an unfinished garage, too scared to move. The sweat that drenched his T-shirt was only partly the result of the fierce heat of the day. It was also fear. If these bad guys caught him, he'd end up as a bonfire. And, he reminded himself, all this mess was nothing to do with him anyway. Wasn't it enough that life had thrown diabetes at him? One minute, he was getting treatment in hospital, feeling safe and secure. The next, he was risking his life by stalking sadistic terrorists. One minute, he'd been arrested by feds. The next, he was virtually working for them. Diabetes and Cassie had turned his life upside down. The old carefree Wayne had gone and the world's first robot-controlled agent had taken his place.

Wayne wanted to ask Cassie if she thought his robots were making him attempt this stupid rescue. He could almost imagine Professor Clayton manipulating a console in the Department of Experimental Medicine, making him move left, right, forward, back, or making him hide inside a garage. Cassie would know if that was possible but, before he could ask her, he needed to find out if she was in the house and, if she was, he had to get her out in one piece.

There was something else that terrified Wayne. The bottle of green pills bulging his trouser pocket and the woman with the smashed face reminded him that there was another reason to find Cassie. After a lifetime of pleasing himself, it came as a shock that he was now concerned for someone else's well-being.

The thought of Cassie losing her face after all she'd gone through stirred him into action. He knew what he had to do, even if it was ludicrously dangerous. Two of the half-built walls of brick and breeze-block were bounded by scaffolding. That was his access to the upstairs of the house. The house wasn't overlooked at the back but he'd be in full view of a neighbour or anyone walking past the front. He thought that, if he acted boldly enough, if he carried a few bricks and swung his shoulders as he went about it, everyone would think he'd been employed to help out with the construction. They might even imagine that he was on a summer holiday job. He just had to hope that a bad guy didn't appear at the window in the wall above the garage.

Wayne had always been a good, wiry climber. He was sure-footed and so light that he could pull himself up easily. He didn't just hold the school record for the number of chin-ups; he demoralized the whole of the chasing pack. Over the years, he'd shinned up plenty of walls, fences and trees. Last time the feds had caught him, he'd been halfway up the security fence around a supermarket warehouse. Now, he felt fitter than he'd ever been before.

He hauled himself up on the steel bars and, at the top, set his feet on the unfinished wall. From there, he could reach the window. It was held shut by a simple latch – not enough to keep Wayne out for long. But he did not dare to poke a blade up behind the wooden frame and flick the lever off its latch. It was just too risky when the terrorists were on the other side with their petrol and cigarette lighters.

That thought gave him the inspiration he needed. Perched on the top of the garage, he was out of sight of the garden shed so his idea had a chance. He clambered back down and then sneaked away from the house and sprinted along to the shops on Pot House Lane. A few minutes later, he was returning with a box of matches. Wayne thought it was funny that he was going to start a fire in the shed where the bad guys had threatened to torch him. He hoped the men would suppose that, after they'd dowsed the shed with petrol, today's blazing sun had set it alight. He also hoped it would create enough of a distraction.

Twice on the way back, Wayne had to stop. His heart was palpitating and he felt sick. Putting it down to nerves, he nipped into the school premises, past the buildings, on to the playing fields and located the back of the terrorists' safe house. He thought that if he avoided its front there would be less chance that they'd see him, so he climbed over the fence at the rear and slipped into the garden shed. He poured some fresh petrol from the can on to the floor and then stood back in the doorway, struck a match and threw it towards the back wall. As soon as he saw that a yellow smoky flame was taking hold, he retreated and, bent double, dashed across the lawn. He avoided the noisy path of stones and threw himself towards the garage. Slumping out of sight, he waited.

Two men's footsteps, crunching on the gravel, came past him. They were so close, Wayne could hear every muttered curse. The tutor shouted, "Damn! The hose is in the shed. There's a couple of buckets in the kitchen." As soon as Wayne thought the men were fully occupied with the fire, rushing from the open kitchen door to the flaming hut with bucketfuls of water, he pulled himself acrobatically up the scaffolding once more. As he swung upwards, he didn't notice that the bottle of pills fell from his pocket, hit the garage floor and rolled under a concrete mixer. Concentrating, he pulled his penknife from his other pocket, shoved the blade under the frame, pushed the lever up and opened the window. Within seconds, he tumbled inside head-first.

He found himself on a landing with three doors. The first led into a bathroom. When he tried the second, he found himself in a bedroom and, much to his relief, Cassie was there. She was bound to the bed and gagged with a bandage. She had her eyes closed, oblivious to the blaze outside.

With his penknife, Wayne cut the straps that held her wrists to the headboard. At once, Cassie opened her eyes and looked startled. Unnecessarily, Wayne put a finger to his lips. Cassie had no choice but to keep quiet.

Wayne didn't want to waste time removing the gag. Instead, he cut the cord from her ankles and then grabbed her hand. "Come on!" he whispered, helping to pull her up. "We're out of here."

He had hoped to tear down the stairs, out of the front door and away at speed but Cassie moved like an old woman whose joints needed oiling.

"Run!" Wayne said, trying to encourage her.

On her feet, Cassie still looked shaky, hesitant and bewildered. Both of her eyes – the real one and the false one – were wide with shock. She had her hands behind her head, fiddling with the knot in the bandage.

"No time for that. They're in the garden. Come on! They'll be back any second." He dragged her by the arm, out on to the landing and down the stairs. He fumbled with the front door lock with one hand and kept hold of Cassie with the other. Round the corner, he could hear running water in the kitchen and raised voices. He just had to hope that the bad guys were too busy to notice him. Finally pushing open the door with his foot, he yanked Cassie out of her prison.

Wayne hadn't anticipated what would happen next. Wind flew into the house and the through-draught slammed the back door shut with a loud bang, alerting Martin and the tutor to Cassie's escape.

Wayne let out a curse then shouted, "Move!" He charged towards Bracken Moor sports ground with Cassie, still gagged, in tow.

A distance behind them, Martin and the tutor were piling into a car. Luckily, it was facing the other way so they lost time as they executed a U-turn. Then, tyres squealing, they set off after Wayne and Cassie.

All the time, Cassie was slowly coming to her wits, shaking off her cramps and moving more freely. Yet, with a bandage across her face, she couldn't breathe easily.

Wayne wasn't feeling great himself. As his adrenalin pumped, he felt more and more fragile. But he also knew their only chance was to keep going. He shouted, "I know where they can't follow us. Come on!" He was still much faster than Cassie, irritated by her sluggishness.

At the end of Kenworthy Road, Wayne used the instinct that frequently kept the police off his back. He turned right, uphill, almost doubling back. He felt sure that the bad guys would assume he'd take the easy option of going downhill towards Manchester Road. He pulled Cassie into a crouching position behind a hedge and held her there in silence, hardly daring to breathe. When he heard the car brake, hesitate at the junction and then screech downhill, he waited another few seconds before jumping up again. "Come on."

He struggled with Cassie up the steep hill and then headed along Broomfield Lane. Halfway to the end, Cassie came to a complete halt. Behind the gag, she was gasping for air. But that wasn't why she'd stopped. She was pointing wildly at a road sign.

"It's only a dead end for cars," Wayne said and tugged her back into motion. Some distance behind them, he could hear alarmingly loud revving and in his head he could hear the words of that fed: "Not to be messed with." By now the bad guys had probably figured out which way they'd gone.

The road fizzled out at the edge of a wood. Wayne didn't stop. He headed down one of the three footpaths into Fox Glen. He reckoned that, even if Martin and the tutor spotted them going into the nature trail, they wouldn't know which track to take through the wooded valley. He jerked Cassie along the shortcut that he used years before to reach the bus route back into Sheffield.

After they'd leaped over the stream, Cassie began to make strangled murmurings from behind her bandage and pointed frantically to her mouth. Looking around and listening to make sure the terrorists weren't bearing down on them, Wayne took pity on her. Shrouded by the closely packed trees, he turned her by her shoulders, cut through the tightly tied gag and threw it away.

Immediately, Cassie coughed and then spat on to the earth. "What are you doing?" she cried.

"Carr Road's up here. We can get a bus."

"A bus? Don't be silly. Let's find a phone box or a house and call the police."

"The police? I didn't think of that." Calling the feds still didn't come naturally to Wayne. "Whatever. Let's move!"

Panting, Cassie said, "OK, but I can't run any more. Walk." After being strapped to a bed for two days, she was out of condition.

"All right. A fast walk." As he went along, Wayne pulled out his mobile. He was about to call that secret security number when the phone rang.

"Yes?" he said cautiously.

"Wayne?"

"Yes."

Again, a man with an English accent did not introduce himself but assumed that Wayne knew who he was. "Where are you?"

"Er . . . Stocksbridge."

"Oh. Can you talk?"

"Well. . ."

"Look, it's important. We've been in touch with Cassie's

father. You tell me exactly where you are and we'll come and get you."

Cassie whispered, "Who is it?"

Wayne hadn't caught the sound of that irritating sniff yet but he guessed who it was. He covered the mouthpiece and replied, "They never say. It's the feds, right enough."

"What sort of accent?"

He shrugged. "Sort-of English. Not Irish, anyway."

The man on the phone said, "You sound breathless. What's going on?"

"I've got Cassie!"

Suspicious, Cassie had heard enough. She grabbed the phone and listened.

"What? Cassie! Right, we're on our way. Tell me where you are."

At once, Cassie threw the mobile angrily into a tree trunk. Broken, it fell into a bush.

Wayne looked aghast. "Hey! What. . .?"

"Sort-of English," Cassie muttered with disdain. "That's an Irishman doing an English accent."

"But. . ."

Cassie was beginning to take charge. "Don't trust anyone. Understand?"

22 SEMTEX

Coming to the edge of the wood, they peered out carefully into Carr Road. A woman about to take her dog for a walk in Fox Glen looked at them suspiciously yet said nothing as she went past, eyeing them as if she thought they were up to no good. A few cars were labouring up the hill or cruising down but none of the drivers and passengers seemed to be on the lookout for an escaped hostage. Cassie had no doubt that the bad guys would be out there somewhere, though. They wouldn't give up till they'd snatched her back.

"What car were they in?"

Wayne shrugged. "Not the blue Astra. It were red. A Golf maybe. I didn't take it in."

"Great," Cassie mumbled to herself. She scratched at her itching cheeks.

Still concealed among the trees, still unsure and tense, Wayne nodded towards her face and asked, "You OK?"

Cassie had a slight rash, not yet full-scale eruptions, on her facial skin. She looked as if she'd been out in the sun too long. On her forehead, there were the first signs of peeling. "I don't know." She frowned, far more troubled than she would admit. "I haven't had any anti-rejection pills."

"It's all right," Wayne replied with a grin and swelling

with pride. "I've got. . ." He put a hand into his pocket. "I went to the hospital." His triumphant expression turned to puzzlement and then to dismay as his desperately probing fingers failed to find the plastic container. "Oh no!"

"What? You got some and then lost them?"

He sighed and muttered, "Suppose. Sorry."

"Sorry?" Cassie snapped. "Is that all you've got to say?" Her hand darted to her threatened face.

"I did. . ." He was going to protest that he had at least rescued her but he gave up. She wasn't in the mood to listen to excuses when her face was decaying slowly. "When a bus comes, we've got to run for it."

"Are you still going on about a bus? And where do you think we're going?"

"Away from here." Brightening, Wayne suggested, "The hospital. I can nick more pills."

Cassie shook her head. "No. Too obvious. Bad guys will be watching. There's not many places we *can* go. The Hillsborough house, ferries or planes to Northern Ireland. They'll have them all covered. They'll be on the lookout by now. That's the miracle of mobiles."

"Yeah, well. I had a mobile a little while ago. I could've called the feds." It was the closest he could come to criticizing Cassie.

"We need a police station."

"You said we don't trust anyone."

"Anyone who contacts us," Cassie replied. "I don't know what we can do apart from going to a police station."

"There's one at the bottom of the road. I've . . . er . . . been there before."

"OK."

Still sheltering in the wood, Wayne warned her, "It's dangerous."

"I know," she said, breaking cover. "But we can't stay here for ever."

Hesitantly, they went out on to the pavement and strode down the hill, expecting the sound of squealing brakes at any moment. Every time a red car drove past, they cringed and glanced fearfully inside but there was no sign of Martin and the tutor. They reached the busy main road at the bottom of the valley without a hitch. The police station was directly opposite but there wasn't a crossing. Standing at the kerb, they waited, looking both ways for a gap in the traffic.

The IFG men were a step ahead of them. Martin had figured it out. "Where are they going to go?" he'd asked with a twisted smile. "The hospital? Their house? No way." He'd parked the Golf just along from the police station on Manchester Road. He'd tapped on the windscreen, his finger towards the police station, and said, "That's where. Sanctuary."

Suddenly, Cassie let out a scream. She was pointing at the two men emerging from a parked red car.

Wayne glanced at them and then stared at the endless passing traffic. Terrorists on one side, safe haven on the other. In between, a death trap of a road. Making up his mind, he opted for the road. At least, if he created a crash, even if he got himself killed, Cassie would be able to dash across to safety in the confusion.

Martin and the tutor were sprinting, matching each other stride for stride, only a few metres away. Their faces were contorted with effort and fury.

His chest on fire, Wayne took a deep breath while the bus went past and then he stepped out. He didn't really see what happened next. There was an unbelievably loud screech. A car spun in front of him and shot across into the oncoming traffic. There was a stomach-churning crunch, followed by a series of bangs. Horns blared briefly and then there was silence. The world had stopped. Even the terrorists pulled up.

Wayne grabbed Cassie's arm and yanked her into the road. As they sped across, Wayne realized they were treading on broken glass and debris. The front of every car littering the street was filled with an inflated air bag. Wayne and Cassie slammed straight into three officers coming out of the police station, alarm on their faces.

"The bad guys are there!" Cassie yelled hysterically, pointing.

"What?"

"There! One's in a baseball cap. You can get them."

More police officers poured out of the building.

Cassie had a policeman firmly by the arm. "Inside, miss," he said. "Come on, now. Let's calm down."

The duty sergeant remained at her post and looked up quizzically at Wayne and Cassie.

"You've got to protect us," Wayne shouted above the commotion.

"From what?"

"The bad guys," Cassie replied. "They're outside. You're going to be under siege any minute."

"You'd better believe it," Wayne added. "Get your shooters out."

"Siege? Guns?" The sergeant laughed. "Where do you think you are? New York? This is Stocksbridge."

"If you don't believe us, make a call." Wayne recited the secret direct line number he'd been given by those plain-clothes feds.

The duty sergeant's face changed abruptly. "How do you know that number? It's a secure. . ." Realizing that these two kids might just be genuine, she said, "Follow me." Down the corridor, she twisted round and added, "I'm going to put you in the interview room till I've got to the bottom of this. What's your names?"

Sitting on opposite sides of the table, Cassie and Wayne listened to the noise that filtered in from outside, mainly sirens. In the windowless room, they weren't sure if they were listening to ambulances, fire engines, police cars or all three. Wayne was fiddling with the recording equipment that, in the past, had taped one of his statements. A little matter of joy-riding in a stolen car.

Cassie stared at Wayne for a while and said, "That was pretty . . . brave. Reckless, but brave."

"Suppose."

"What did they do to you?"

"Who?"

"The bad guys."

"Nothing."

Cassie nodded. Martin had been playing games again when he'd told her that Wayne had betrayed her. "Are you all right? You look very pale."

"I'm not the only one." He wasn't going to complain

about feeling empty and incredibly weak. He wasn't going to mention the mother of all headaches. He couldn't expect anything else.

Cassie nodded. "I didn't thank you for getting me out."

Wayne shrugged and leaned back more on the seat. He'd never felt out of harm's way in a police station before. So, despite his frailty and faintness, he was relaxed. "No problem," he said in a tone that James Bond might have used. "Just tell me one thing."

"What?"

"What *did* the inflatable teacher say to the inflatable student who was naughty because he took a pin into the inflatable school?"

Cassie grinned. "Ah, you know about inflatable now?"

"I looked it up, like."

"Well, the teacher said, 'You've let me down and you've let the whole school down but, much worse, you've let yourself down.'"

It was then, when almost all of the police officers at the station were outside dealing with the multiple pile-up, that the bad guys made their move. The whole of the outside wall on Wayne's left blew up and collapsed. Along with a thick plume of pulverized plaster, Wayne and Cassie were thrown across the room and slammed into the opposite wall.

Searching through the wreckage, trampling over bricks and cement, the bad guys spotted Cassie and dragged their stunned hostage away.

If they saw Wayne, lying inert in the dust, his blood leaking liberally, they didn't take any notice. Maybe they still wanted him on the outside as their intermediary or perhaps they had no further use for him. More likely, they thought he was dying.

ADRENALIN 23

After the treatment, Arthur felt about half his real age. Blood surged afresh through his honed arteries. He was like a reconditioned car – serviced, polished and restored to its original condition – and he had his foot down on the accelerator. He was putting his invigorated body through its paces. Feeling like a young man again, he demanded the same in his women. He wouldn't be seen with haggard sixty year olds. They wouldn't be able to keep up with him and they certainly wouldn't do anything for his image or his ego. He went for the girls under thirty-five. That way, he'd be all over the newspapers, admired for staying attractive and virile. Oh, yes. He intended to make full use of his improved blood flow. He intended to feel the rush of adrenalin over and over again.

It was when he reached the height of passion with one of his glamorous gold-diggers that Arthur suffered a complete, catastrophic and embarrassing collapse.

Professor Richard Clayton shook his head. "It's adrenalin that's the problem," he said, downcast. "I've checked and, under normal circumstances, the nanorobots are fine. Absolutely fine. But for some reason – I don't know why yet – they're unstable in high concentrations of adrenalin."

Hilary had her own medical problems but, even so, she couldn't resist a smile. "So," she said, "you can make people young again but they've got to avoid excitement."

Richard nodded.

"Makes you wonder what the point of feeling young is."

"I admit it's . . . ironic."

"What happens?"

"The robots seem to think they're in a foreign environment when they're swimming in all that adrenalin so they start attacking . . . well, almost anything. They went for Arthur's heart. He's going to be fine but he's had a coronary."

"What does it mean for Wayne Wingate?"

"I'm not sure," Richard confessed. "I haven't seen him regularly. Back to his old unreliable ways of missing appointments. You'll remember last time he was in."

"Mmm. The case of the missing pills," Hilary murmured pensively, thinking of Cassie. "Worrying."

"If . . . when he gets excited, he's not going to feel good. But I don't know exactly what'll happen. His diabetes will be fine. It's not those robots that're playing up. It's the others. They'll think there's something wrong with him because of all the adrenalin and they'll attack whatever they think is causing it. But he's young and fit, not like Arthur. His body will fight back. I doubt if he'll collapse quite so dramatically."

"Let's hope not." She shook her head. "Given that you didn't get permission for his anti-ageing treatment, you're in a mess. Not as big a mess as Wayne, of course. You ought to be trying to find him."

"I'm a medic, not a private detective. But I am trying to come up with a way of reversing the process and getting rid of the robots. Not easy, but nowhere near as tricky as reversing a failing face transplant," said Richard. "How is Cassie O'Rourke – minus immunosuppressants? Or has Wayne become her unofficial supplier?"

Annoyed, Hilary shuffled uneasily. "I hope not. He took ones I'd modified specifically for Dorothy Heywood when she wasn't responding to normal treatment. I don't know how Cassie would react to them. I'm expecting her to turn up in panic as soon as she starts to show the first signs of rejection. It'll be anytime now."

"She'd better. Losing one face, you can put down to a unique set of circumstances. Two begins to look like carelessness or a trend."

"OK, OK. All we're saying is, any medical advance comes at a price. It always did and we're both learning it always will."

The Northern General's Accident and Emergency Ward was in overdrive, dealing with the casualties from the Stocksbridge incident. The broken bones, whiplash injuries, and cuts and bruises were shelved while medics raced through reception with a victim in a critical condition. Alongside, a paramedic was shouting what he'd discovered at the scene and in the ambulance. "Severe shock from class four haemorrhage. External and internal bleeding. Abdominal swelling probably means the explosion ruptured some blood vessels. Airway cleared. Two IV lines in place. We put him on plasma and dextran but circulation's failing.

Heartbeat and blood pressure are way down. He's cold and clammy. Pupils dilated." None of them knew that the pallid boy at the point of death was also a very special human being. Absorbed in their attempts to bring him back from the brink, to maintain a blood flow, the trauma team had no time to consult his files, no reason to consult the Department of Experimental Medicine. They knew only that they had four minutes to resuscitate him before his brain suffered irreversible damage.

To staunch the haemorrhaging, a nurse was applying pressure to an ugly gash across his abdomen, and another three nurses were taping up separate wounds in his arms and thigh. "Whole blood and lots of it," a doctor yelled. "Have we got a type yet?"

"Coming."

"OK. One litre hypertonic saline now. And plasma."

The team worked on him like Formula One engineers completing a well-rehearsed pit-stop.

"Oxygen supplement, please," the doctor requested.

"We're losing his pulse."

"External blood loss more-or-less under control."

"He's about to go."

"He's bleeding internally. One shot of intravenous vasopressin."

"Done."

"Standby for emergency thoracotomy on my say-so if it comes to that."

"We have cardiac arrest."

"OK. Stand back." The doctor applied the paddles to Wayne's inert chest. "Clear." But the sudden jolt of electricity did not waken his spent heart. "Again." The doctor waited for a few seconds. "Well?"

"He's. . . Yep. He's back with us."

There was an audible sigh of relief from the team. They had restarted Wayne's heart but only Wayne himself could provide the will to keep it going.

"Respiration and systolic blood pressure coming back up slowly."

While they waited for their patient to stabilize, the medics began to repair the worst wounds in his thigh and abdomen. The doctor examined him closely for signs of further damage. "Once we're done here, he'll need CT scanning and radiography. He might have some broken bones as well."

"He's type O rhesus-positive."

"Good. Start blood transfusion right away. But I want his cardiac output up. We'll try adrenalin."

"Where am I?" Cassie's words seemed to hammer inside her skull and she groaned. It felt like the worst sort of hangover. She could hardly bear to budge her delicate head and she felt nauseous. She expected to be sick every time she made the slightest movement.

Martin laughed at her discomfort and then shook his head, making a tutting noise. "Well, if you will do a runner, what can you expect?"

Cassie twisted her neck to the left so that she could see Martin clearly. "Where?" she whispered insistently.

"Not in Stocksbridge, for sure." He opened his arms wide and said, "Guess."

161

It was some sort of filthy workshop. Rusting exhaust systems and other vehicle parts were lying around on the oil-soaked concrete base. All sorts of tools were hung on the walls, alongside peeling paint. There were sturdy wooden benches around the sides and overhead there was a corrugated iron roof. The only light came from a couple of camping gas lamps. "A garage."

Martin grinned. "Give the girl a gold star."

Ignoring his sarcasm, Cassie asked, "What happened? I can't. . . I don't remember."

"You escaped, we brought you back. That's all." He scratched at his head, knocking his baseball cap to one side. "In fact, we owe you. Your aborted flight gave us the opportunity to show how much you mean to us. Now, everyone knows we mean business."

This time, Cassie's hands were bound together with a plastic tie. By lifting them both, though, she could touch her face. Near her ears, she could feel some swelling and cold skin. The cuts on her cheeks were a result of shrapnel and not rejection, but they showed no sign of healing. Her shoulders and legs ached relentlessly. Under her clothing, she was probably a mass of bruises. Her injuries, the dust that clung to every part of her, and the grit in her mouth refreshed her confused memory. "Did you really blow up the police station?"

"That's over-the-top," the surly tutor replied. "I took out one wall, no more. Just enough."

"Where's Wayne?"

Martin shrugged.

"Have you got him?"

"You know, I admire him. Plucky lad. No, we didn't take him."

"So, where is he?"

"Heaven, hell or hospital. Take your pick."

Cassie looked aghast.

"Last time I saw him, he looked rough to say the least," Martin explained. "But those clever doctors will probably pull something out the bag again. Maybe he's not due to meet his maker just yet."

Out there in the real world, Cassie had as much freedom as the police would allow, as well as her new face, access to anti-rejection pills, and a real friend in Wayne. Inside, held by the bad guys, she'd have none of those things. Her ankles were tethered to a massive worn tyre that had come off a bus or a lorry or a tractor. Even a fit Cassie would not have been able to pick it up and run with it. "I need a shower," she said softly.

"You're welcome to have one," Martin replied, "if you can spot one."

Over Martin's shoulder, the tutor added, "You might be in luck if it rains."

"A drink, then." Her throat was dry, the dust irritated her lungs and her mouth felt like sandpaper.

Martin nodded and the tutor put a bottle of water on the floor within her reach.

"You haven't gagged me this time," she remarked.

"I'll save you a lot of effort, flower," said Martin. "It's a disused garage in the middle of nowhere. There's no one around. You can shout if you want but. . ." He shrugged. "It's pointless."

Cassie took a swig from the bottle, turned her head, coughed and vomited on to the concrete.

BLOOD 24

With their patient out of danger, the A and E staff had at last had time to consult Wayne Wingate's medical record. Several of them had not even heard of nanomedicine until they read that it had put his diabetes to rest. Finding themselves out of their depth, they'd called the Department of Experimental Medicine.

Professor Clayton was glancing through the notes on his patient when his eyebrows rose in alarm. "You gave him adrenalin?"

"His heart needed stimulating."

"Right. I want another blood transfusion. A complete replacement."

"What?"

"It's nothing to do with his injuries. I need to clean out as many nanorobots as possible and then deal with the ones that're left before they reproduce themselves. He mustn't have any food or nutrients."

"What are you trying to do? Starve him to death? It won't take long. There's not a scrap of fat on him."

"No," Richard responded. "Starve his nanorobots to death."

The trauma doctor shook his head. "I'm not going to sanction that. He's already frail. You'll take him too close to the edge."

"I don't see a choice."

"Look, we don't have the resource—"

"Transfer him into my care, then."

The doctor turned away, hesitated and let out a long breath before answering. "All right. We can always use another bed."

Wayne was lucky. He'd lost more than half of his blood, he had a body covered in bruises, but he was alive and he'd not broken any bones. His heart and kidney had not failed. Richard suspected that the only reason his nanorobots had not finished him off when they found themselves in a strange adrenalin-rich environment was that so few of them remained in his body. Wayne had spilled most of them along with his blood and, without food to fuel their replication, they were not yet back up to strength. If they were allowed to rally, they would not just impede his recovery but threaten his weakened heart and kidneys.

Wayne's misfortune provided Richard with a fantastic opportunity to study the reaction of nanorobots in severe conditions. If he had cared only about medical science and not about the patient, Wayne's battered body would have made an ideal test-tube for the experiment. Richard would have been keen to monitor the robots as they recovered from the shock to their host. After the volume of blood Wayne had lost, the nanorobots would be down to very low numbers and, with Wayne so weak and lacking in food, it would have been fascinating to find out how quickly they got back up to strength. But Richard couldn't detach his scientific curiosity from his concern for a sick boy.

Wayne's misfortune also provided Richard with a

wonderful opportunity to flush out as many nanorobots as possible by a blood exchange, kill the rest by depriving them of fuel and, as long as starvation killed the robots before it killed Wayne, start again with just the remedy for diabetes. If his idea worked, he'd remove the anti-ageing robots from Arthur in the same way. He couldn't allow people to wander around with unmanageable, rampaging robots inside them every time their adrenalin levels rose. Already, Richard had had enough of cosmetic treatments. After Wayne and Arthur, he had resolved never to go down that road again.

Martin took a long hard look at the left side of Cassie's face and exclaimed, "Hey, you've got a false eye. That explains why you're always looking at me at a funny angle. So, modern medicine hasn't got around to transplanting eyes or making new ones yet." As he moved around peering at her, the peak of his cap was once more annoyingly close to her skin. "You weren't kidding when you said there was something wrong, were you? Your face doesn't look healthy – a bit brown here and there. Withering petals."

Cassie shrugged.

Martin pulled back. "Doesn't bother me. Plenty of times I've caught live fish with dead bait." He extracted a mobile from his leather jacket. "It just takes a phone call."

"Who to?" asked Cassie, curious about Martin's scheming.

"Whoever answers Wayne's phone."

"No one will. I broke it."

Martin smiled, shook his head and tutted like an exasperated teacher. "Temper tantrum, eh? After hearing me pretending to be your father's keepers. It was worth a try to get you back without wasting perfectly good Semtex but I was never any good at an English accent. No matter. The police'll divert any calls to that number. Right now, they'll be waiting for me to get through to them."

Cassie watched him keying the number. He was amazingly cool, like a man in total command of the situation. He smiled confidently at her while he waited for an answer.

"You have ninety seconds of my time," he said, not bothering with the niceties of an introduction. "But that's enough because you already know what I want and what I'm offering in exchange."

He listened for a moment and then said, "She's got a few bruises but she's OK."

Martin sighed impatiently so the police officer at the other end could hear. "I'd let Wayne come in to check she's here and well. Is he alive? . . .Yeah? Tough kid. Anyway, if he's . . . inconvenienced, the traitor can see his daughter when he gives himself up . . .All right. I'll allow her four words."

Martin assumed that Cassie could figure out the conversation from hearing one side of it. He knelt beside her and held the phone in front of her mouth. "Show them you're alive."

"I'm OK," Cassie blurted out in a trembling voice, "but tell. . ."

Martin took the phone away and admonished her. "That's your word quota. You wasted fifty per cent. Still, it's up to you." Into the mobile, he said, "That's *your* lot as well.

168

I'll be in touch. Next time, I want news that Wayne's standing by or the traitor's coming. Whichever." He put the phone away. "It's all plain sailing from here as long as they play the game."

"What about Wayne?"

"He was banging on death's door for a bit apparently but no one let him in. Indestructible, it seems. He's off the danger list now, slacking in a hospital bed, too lazy to be our go-between any more. I guess he's distracted by all those gorgeous nurses whose faces aren't falling to pieces."

Cassie tried not to get upset by his taunting. She didn't know if the knots in her stomach were the result of Martin's stifling presence, her worsening health or something to do with being scared silly. She still felt queasy, she'd developed an irritating tic just below her right eye, and the itching around her face was becoming unbearable. At least now she could scratch it but she suspected that a nurse would tell her that she shouldn't. The traces of blood under her fingernails told her the same thing. She also suspected that the unpleasant tingling would soon turn to pain.

"You probably don't know," Martin said, "but it's late. We've got three mattresses – pure luxury – so we're all going to kip down here, nice and friendly." He watched the expression of distaste develop on Cassie's face and grinned at her. "After your misguided bid for freedom, you can't expect privacy any more."

Lying there in her dirty clothes with no blanket, Cassie tried to make her sobs silent. She longed to be ordinary again. That's all. She thought back to a time before her dad turned the world upside down. As a young girl, she would

169

stare into a mirror and see the imperfections in her appearance but now she realized there was nothing wrong at all with what nature had given her. When she shut her eye, she used her memory to reconstruct that face and it looked nice. If only she could have it back. That's what she wanted most. Along with her own face, she needed her home, family and freedom. But, one by one, they'd all been destroyed by Martin. Only her dad remained safe and sound. But not for much longer.

For Cassie O'Rourke's sake, and for his own sake, Richard caved in when Hilary Staunton demanded to see Wayne. His patient wasn't well enough to see anyone but Richard couldn't refuse Hilary. He recognized that she needed to ask him about Cassie. He also recognized that Hilary could easily have him struck off because he had carried out an unauthorized procedure on Wayne.

Sitting beside his bed, Hilary leaned towards his ear and asked gently, "What's happening to Cassie, Wayne? What's going on?"

He looked even more scrawny than usual. He was pale and inert. And he was silent.

Hilary tried again. "I'm Professor Staunton, Wayne, and I need to know where Cassie is."

A low moan came from Wayne's lips but there was nothing like a sensible response.

"Can you hear me, Wayne? This is important, really important. Cassie trusts you. You've got to help me to help her. Even if you can't tell me anything else, is she taking her pills?"

His eyes remained shut but he breathed in as if summoning strength. "No," he mumbled.

Hilary's heart leaped. "No?"

"No."

"Why not?" she said urgently. "What's going on? Where is she?"

But Wayne had withdrawn into himself again.

Even though Hilary knew she wasn't going to get anything more from him, she continued to sit there in the private room, shocked. She felt anxious for her patient and fearful for her work. She was angry. Ever since Cassie had left the department and gone off with this tearaway, things had gone downhill. To repay Hilary's painstaking investment in Cassie's face, the girl *had* to keep taking her medication. Not a lot to ask. Then Cassie would have her flawless face and Hilary would have an advertisement to lure wealthy clients. Before Cassie's disappearing act, Hilary had even been thinking about presenting her to the press as a picturesque surgical breakthrough, a miracle cure. Following the difficulties with Dorothy Heywood, Hilary needed a boost but everything seemed to be conspiring against her.

The more she thought about it, the more livid she became with this turn of events. She cursed under her breath and left.

"You don't look much like police," Richard Clayton said, looking up and down at the three men who had come into the department.

"No, not regulars. We're in the security force." The one

who spoke pinched his nose between forefinger and thumb and then sniffed as if he'd got some sort of sinus problem.

"And you want a word with Wayne Wingate?"

"Yes."

"Not a chance," Richard responded.

"He may have vital information—"

"If he has, he's not in a position to give it." After giving in to Hilary Staunton, he wasn't having his ailing patient disturbed again.

"We have to establish if he can come—"

Once again, Richard cut in. "He can't. He's a very poorly boy. He's died twice already. Once at the collapsed police station – the paramedics resuscitated him – and once in A and E where a trauma team revived him. That's quite a strain on a body. He won't be going anywhere for a while." He didn't intend to tell them that Wayne's therapy was making him worse before it stood a chance of making him better.

Another of the three men stepped forward. "Look, I'm Cassie O'Rourke's father—"

The two security men grimaced disapprovingly. The one with the sniff interrupted. "Don't say any—"

O'Rourke ignored them. "I really need to see Wayne. He's spoken to my daughter and he probably knows what her kidn—"

This time the other police officer stepped in. "No," he said firmly. "We can't discuss anything at the moment."

"Seeing Wayne won't help anyway," Richard replied. "He's unconscious and he'll be that way for some time. Leave me a number and I'll let you know when you can come back and hope to get something out of him. In the meantime, you should catch a word with Professor Staunton. You could update her on what's happening. She's concerned that Cassie hasn't been in to continue her medicine."

"You mean, she hasn't been taking the anti-rejection pills?" O'Rourke looked horrified.

"Well," Richard answered, "you'd have to speak to Professor Staunton but I understand she'll have run out of tablets by now."

"But she could lose. . ." O'Rourke's hand shot to his own face.

Richard nodded. "I'm sorry."

Realizing that Cassie was in greater danger from her own antibodies than from the bad guys, O'Rourke took a deep breath and made up his mind. "Where do I find Professor Staunton? She's got to give me the pills. I'm going to see Cassie very soon."

25 EXPLOSIVES

Martin looked astounded for the first time. Wearing a frown, genuinely puzzled, he exclaimed, "Why? You ask me why?"

Cassie nodded. "Yes. Why are you doing this?"

"I'll tell you," he said, his voice strident, angry. "My mother, she lived in Short Strand. Three thousand Catholics surrounded by sixty thousand Protestants who want the place to themselves. They nailed notices to the trees outside the shops saying, *No Catholics Served*. The loyalist mural painted on the end of the terrace has got *No Short Strand Taigs on Our Road* written underneath it. Over the top it says, *We'll never let go of Ulster*. The lamppost at the end of Mam's road had a printed note tied to it: *Taigs enter at their own risk*. Union flags and streamers everywhere. You know what? She's passed away now." He shook his head in misery and bewilderment. "The chemist wouldn't sell her the tablets she needed. He'd been threatened by loyalist paramilitaries and told not to serve Catholics. He wouldn't even sell them to the community nurse because everyone knew she'd volunteered to get prescriptions for everyone, Catholic or Protestant. When Mam was too ill to walk, they poured petrol though her letter box and set her house alight. Then the ambulance and fire engines couldn't get through because the Protestants knew they were heading for a Catholic home and stoned them."

"Yeah. I know," Cassie muttered softly. "I had to fight to get to school. It all starts with a couple of women – a Catholic and a Protestant – having a silly argument in the Co-op and minutes later, five hundred are out on the street, knocking down walls with hammers to get bricks as ammunition and the kids are going door-to-door for empties to make fire bombs. I've seen it. But what's that got to do with you kidnapping me?"

"Don't be naïve. If Catholics don't stick together, what hope is there? There's only one thing worse than a loyalist and that's a Catholic who turns on his own kind."

"Dad didn't. He turned on violence, that's all. He was Republican through and through. Always was, always will be. But he thought you were ruining the cause. He thought our best chance was the peace process."

Martin tutted as if in pity at a child who couldn't understand. "Remember what they say: *We'll never let go of Ulster.*"

"If it's painted on a wall, it must be true, eh?"

"I'll tell you what the Good Friday Agreement is. It's surrender. No. The war goes on. It's the only way. And in a war, no one tolerates a traitor."

Cassie was drenched in sweat. The neglected workshop was sweltering but she also suspected that she had a fever. Her heart seemed to be galloping. On her face, she thought that she could feel a few blisters and open cuts. After probing her skin, she noticed that her fingertips smelled horrible. She didn't know exactly what was happening but the signs weren't good. Her face was beginning to scare her more even than a crazed terrorist. Plucking up her courage, she retorted, "Well, I'm sorry, but killing me and Dad won't bring your mother back."

She closed her eye and steeled herself for a reprisal, expecting a slap or a punch or at least a sharp word, but nothing came. When she dared to look again, Martin was simply staring at her absently. He wasn't going to punish her but he wasn't going to change his heart and let her go either. Cassie guessed that he was wondering if he'd embarked on his personal crusade for wider political reasons or simply because his mother had been blighted by anti-Catholic fervour.

Cassie continued pointedly, "At least you know how I feel. *Someone* murdered my mum."

"There's no comparison," Martin stated bluntly.

"Oh? How's that?"

"My mother hadn't done anything. You and your mother, you harboured a traitor."

"That's a hanging offence, is it?"

"Yes."

Cassie could hear the constant sinister hiss of camping gas. Behind Martin, the tutor was working quietly at a bench with one of the lanterns burning brightly at his elbow. He seemed to be hunched over some sort of leather strap. She did not dare to guess what he was doing but she shivered whenever she looked in his direction.

She found his silence ominous. She really wanted to ask him the same question. Why was he a terrorist? What drove him to do what he did? But she was too intimidated.

The tutor didn't care about politics in Ireland or anywhere

else. He wasn't against one side or the other. He was against the world for the lousy hand he'd been dealt. He cared only about explosives and so he adored anyone who gave him the opportunity to make them and use them.

It started when he was at school in Dublin. He'd seen a demonstration of metals reacting with water. Lithium was boring, sodium flamed and fizzed when a piece the size of a pea hit the liquid. Then he was shown video clips of more dangerous experiments. A tiny pellet of potassium burned angrily with a purple flame. The reaction of rubidium with water fascinated him and brought a huge smile to his face because, when the metal touched the water, it exploded with a massive bang. Behind a safety screen, the tank holding the water smashed immediately. Shards of glass flew in all directions and water cascaded out of the splintered container.

At once, the ashen schoolboy was captivated. Such a ridiculous amount of power stored in a small piece of metal, waiting for water to release it. From that moment, he knew what he wanted to do with the rest of his life. He smuggled a large chunk of sodium out of the Science Preparation Room at the end of the day and went down to the lake. Standing on the bridge, he dropped the metal into the calm water and watched it skim spectacularly over the surface, frightening ducks and killing fish, riding on a blazing raft of hydrogen gas.

For a while he worked in a fireworks factory but he was dismissed when he got too adventurous and his rockets evolved from stunning to hazardous. A few days after his departure, the whole factory was alight in a noisy and dazzling display of uncontrolled pyrotechnics. The place burned down with firecrackers exploding, rockets flying everywhere, Catherine wheels spinning into the air, Roman candles spraying light. It was a brilliant show but two workers were killed and several residents nearby were injured.

The police were desperate to detain the aggrieved ex-worker so that he could assist them with their inquiries into the arson. In Ireland, though, it was easy to find an organization that would shield him from the authorities in exchange for the use of his talents. He disappeared, got a new identity, and then left for Sheffield in England where he was sleeper for the IFG, occasionally called upon to assist in a job.

He was bright and knowledgeable. In Sheffield he could do almost anything but the men who worked his strings wanted him in a secure and respectable profession. He went into teaching but that wasn't what he really wanted to do. He lived for the coded messages from Ireland that requested explosives. He never thought of the things and people he might hurt when he handed over another new bomb. They never entered into his equation. They were nothing compared with the awesome earth-shattering beauty of explosions.

"I'm going in," O'Rourke stated.

"No," his minder from the security force replied. "We haven't got it worked out properly yet."

"You heard the doctor. She said she didn't know how long Cassie had got. As little as three days, maybe. And it's not just a matter of her face. We're talking about her life!"

"We've got to think about your life as well."

"There's no argument. Next time Martin calls," O'Rourke said, "agree to everything. I'm going in."

"At what cost?"

"Look. I love my daughter. She's the only thing I've got left. I got her into this – it's my fault – so I'm going to get her safe."

The officer shook his head. "Going in without a decent plan of action won't get her safe. You'll just get yourself killed. And then what will Martin do? Say, 'OK, I'm satisfied now. I'm going to turn over a new leaf. Here's Cassie O'Rourke, safe and sound'? Martin hasn't got the reputation he's got by keeping his word and being a thoroughly decent bloke beneath a hard exterior. He's hard all the way through – like rock. Heart of stone."

"I don't care. She's my daughter."

The policeman rubbed his nose with his hand. "When it comes down to it, you're a member of the public. You can do what you want within the law. I can't stop you. All I can do is advise and I say it's far too risky."

"She's my daughter," O'Rourke repeated.

"If you're dead set. . ."

"I am."

The officer sighed his disapproval and shrugged. Reluctantly, he said, "OK. We know the demands. Wayne told us. No snipers and we can't conceal a weapon on you or fit you with a transmitter."

"I've never used or wanted to use any sort of weapon."

"You'd make an exception for Martin, surely," he replied,

sniffing noisily. "I know I would in your shoes. I'd gladly despatch him with anything I could lay my hands on. You'd save a lot of people that way."

O'Rourke shook his head resolutely. "It's wrong. You don't fight fire with fire."

"Well, it doesn't matter. You and me, we don't have to agree. The first thing he'll do is search you head to toe so you can't carry anything anyway. Until the phone call comes in telling us where and when, let's think about our options. Not that we've got many. I'll call in the whole team in case somebody else's got any bright ideas."

He was a little boy. He was supposed to be at junior school so his age was probably measured in single figures. He was walking home – or going to the place his uncle and auntie called home – with his hands cupped carefully together, forming a cage. Occasionally he smiled as tiny feathers and claws tickled his palms. Now and again, he stopped, pulled his thumbs apart slightly and peered inside. It was still there, still alive.

He couldn't unlock the back door without opening the cage so instead he kicked one of the wooden panels with his foot.

It was his aunt who let him in. "What's this, Wayne?" she muttered, nodding towards the ball that his hands were making.

"A baby bird."

"What?" she exclaimed.

"A bird. A tiny one. It were by a hedge, on the ground. Couldn't fly."

"What's that got to do with you?"

"I can look after it, make it grow, like," Wayne answered with a wide grin.

"The bird's mum's the one to do that."

"It'd been . . . you know . . . left."

"Abandoned."

"Yeah," said Wayne, gazing wide-eyed at his auntie. "Its mummy abandoned it."

"You should've left it by the hedge, silly bugger. Its mum would've come back to sort it out."

"Would she?" Wayne didn't believe it.

"Well, you're not bringing it in here, anyhow," his aunt replied. "I'm not taking another stray in."

Wayne's happy face disappeared. "But I could make a nest for it and feed it. . ."

"Feed it on what?"

Wayne shrugged. "Milk?"

"You'd probably kill it. Real mothers know what to feed their babies."

"But some don't want to," Wayne said, now close to tears.

"Take it back where you found it, Wayne, and hope you haven't scared the mother into not coming back to take care of it."

"But you haven't even seen it." He began to unravel his hands.

"No! It'll get out. I do know what little birds look like."

"But. . ."

"Just take it back, Wayne." She almost pushed him – together with the pathetic creature – back out of the door. "Go on. Sooner the better."

With a heavy heart and heavy legs, Wayne trudged back down the road, trying hard not to cry. He was sure he could've raised the newborn bird and he was equally certain that its mummy had deserted it. Suddenly he had a bright idea, turned round and returned to the house. Checking that his auntie wasn't looking out of the kitchen window, he slipped into the back garden. Putting the bewildered, frightened creature on the ground near the back wall, he scooped out a hollow in the soil and then gently placed the bird in it. "Stay there a minute," he whispered.

He went indoors and his aunt shouted, "Back already?"

"It were only a few doors down," he lied. Wayne dashed upstairs and looked in the bathroom cabinet. He was sure. . . Yes. There was a tiny plastic bottle of eye-drops. Every night, his aunt held the bottle over his uncle's upturned face and squeezed two drops into each eye. Taking the bottle to the sink, Wayne emptied out the medicine and washed the container with water. Then he nipped downstairs and, when his aunt went into the living room, he dashed to the fridge and poured milk hastily into the bottle. Wiping up the milk that he'd spilled, he went back out into the garden, ready to feed his adopted stray.

But it had gone. It wasn't cowering in the dip in the earth. Amazed, and glum because he'd been denied the opportunity of nursing the vulnerable creature, Wayne looked all around the miniature garden. There was no sign of the hatchling. Glancing over the wall, though, he saw his neighbour's self-satisfied cat walking across the lawn. A weedy feather was still clinging to one of its front paws.

Lying in the Department of Experimental Medicine,

knowing that Professor Clayton and the nurses were watching over him, doing lots of things to him, Wayne felt empty. He didn't care. He wasn't sure if he could speak to them but he didn't even try. He was too exhausted. He simply replayed his life while he still had the chance.

26 SWEAT

Martin bent down, snipped through the plastic tie that bound Cassie's hands together and then stood up again. "Take your top off," he ordered.

Cassie recoiled from the threatening figure looming over her. "No."

"Take it off."

"Why?"

"Because if you don't," Martin said, now in a good-humoured voice, "I'll kill you."

"What are you going to do to me?"

"Nothing like you think."

Mistrustful, but too frightened to argue or fight, she slipped out of her T-shirt.

"Stand up."

Warily, racked with abdominal pain, she got to her feet. Her body was mottled with fading bruises from the explosion. If fever had not already made her cheeks hot, she would have been reddening with both anger and embarrassment. She loathed showing herself in trousers and bra to such a beast. She was shaking and sweating profusely.

"Right," said Martin. "We've got a fashion accessory for you. A new and trendy belt. All the top people are wearing it against their bare midriff so I'm sure you'll want to do the same. It's very fetching. Very sexy."

When Cassie saw the tutor lifting the belt from the workbench and coming towards her, she shrieked, stepped back and fell over the gigantic tyre. Her left hand slapped down in her own vomit.

The tutor looked offended as if she'd insulted his greatest work of art by recoiling from it.

Martin tutted at her. "Oh, come on. It's not that bad. Where's your dignity and bottle? We all have to make sacrifices for our appearance. And I want your appearance to make a big statement."

Cassie wiped her palm on the dirty floor and clambered back unsteadily to her feet.

As Martin took the belt from the tutor, he said to Cassie, "You know, you smell to high heaven. Spot on when you think about it. Your dad was a festering wound among his countrymen and now you're one big festering wound yourself. Yes. I like that. Just deserts."

Cassie inhaled deeply and held the breath to stop herself screaming as Martin passed the bulky strap round her waist. His touch was like the slithering of a snake. She didn't utter a sound but she squirmed as he adjusted the buckle at the front and the horrid thing tightened on her skin. Of course, she didn't need Martin to explain what it was. The punishment belt had five sticks of explosives and a detonator attached to it.

After the bad guy was satisfied with its position, he allowed her to put her shirt back on and then he clamped her hands together again with another tie. This time, he secured them behind her back.

Sweat was trickling over the open wounds on Cassie's

face, more meandered down her arms and there was a torrent of the stuff down her back, soaking into her trousers. It was six days since she'd taken an anti-rejection pill and her immune system was on a very short fuse. She could not see the blisters, oozing wounds and purple swollen patches plastering her face. Right now, the explosive around her waist was more evident and bloodcurdling than the internal bomb. She looked down at the contraption encircling her, already wet with her perspiration, and whispered, "What if I take it off?"

Martin smiled. "Did you ever see that film, *Speed*? The bus blew up if it dropped below fifty miles an hour. Well, this belt's got a heat sensor in it. At body temperature, the switch stays off and there's no boom. You're so hot, you'll be fine. If you take the belt off, the temperature drops and. . ." His clasped hands flew apart and he made a noise like a bomb. He was excited by the prospect, the ingenuity and the cruelty. Deliberately, he walked away from her and took a device, like a remote control for a TV, from a bench. Turning back towards her, he announced, "Of course, I can always override the mechanism with this. Simple *on* button. It's not activated now but, who knows, I could change my mind any time. Though, I'd put a bit of distance between us before I press it. Anyway, it's best if you behave yourself."

Cassie wilted. She slumped gently to the floor, scared in case she set anything off.

Martin laughed aloud at her. "You look like you're settling on to a nest of eggs, trying not to break them! It's all right, gorgeous. Impact won't detonate it." He paused before adding, "And why do you think I've tied your hands behind your back? You're an intelligent girl. Right now, you'll be wondering if you can turn yourself into a suicide bomber, taking out the two of us and saving the traitor. You can't. We thought about it as well. With your hands behind you, you can't take the belt off and trigger an explosion. It needs an electric signal from the zapper or the temperature sensor."

Cassie glared at him with her throbbing eye but she was too upset to speak.

Taking out his mobile, Martin said, "Anyway, time to contact the cops, I think. They might want to hear your voice and I'm not sure how much longer you're going to be able to speak. You're baking so you could pass out on me soon." While he waited for a response to the ringing, he said, "There is some good news. Your false eye is fresh as a daisy. It's only the rest that's. . ." He hesitated, listening for a few seconds to a voice in his ear. "Yes, it's me. Time we got an act together." He paused for a moment before getting impatient. "Hang on. You seem to think we're negotiating. We're not. I'm going to tell you what we're doing. You get Cassie back alive in return for her father. No strings attached. No wires or mobiles either. And none of your men with him." Martin went quiet again, listening. "She's fine. Well . . . maybe fine's exaggerating. I'm looking at her now and she's alive. Now, the place for the exchange. I've got a lovely spot in the hills. Isolated and scenic. . . A doctor?" Martin chuckled. "You know I won't have that. You could send anyone and say it's a doctor. If you want Cassie O'Rourke to get medical attention, you go along with me, no messing, and you have her back. Then she can have as

187

many doctors as you want. She can have a whole hospital to herself. If you want to check she's still on this earth, it'll have to be someone I know: the traitor himself or Wayne Wingate. No one else. And you'd better be quick about it. She's going downhill. . . Pills? Not now. No pills. She gets all the pills she wants when I get O'Rourke." There was a short gap before Martin replied, "Sure. I can give her another four words."

When Martin held out the phone for her, Cassie swallowed. This time, she was expecting it and she'd thought about what to say. "Happy birthday, Dad. I'm. . ."

"Very touching," Martin said, talking to both the policeman and Cassie. "Here's the deal. Last minute, I'll give you precise coordinates and you'll close a road or two."

The British Intelligence officer sniffed and shrugged. "If Wayne Wingate's conscious, we can use him."

Richard Clayton was feeling better at last. He was feeling that he'd reclaimed the moral high ground. He was also shaking his head. "Conscious, yes. But still very poorly. He's not going anywhere." Wayne's last blood test had shown no nanomedical activity at all. The robots in his bloodstream had died before Wayne himself succumbed to the starvation treatment. Now, nurses were pumping nutrition back into him and Richard was about to reintroduce the nanorobots that would control his diabetes.

"I think Wayne should make that decision," said the security officer.

"He's not competent to make it so I'm doing it on his behalf."

"Ah yes. You're good at making decisions on behalf of someone else – without telling them."

Richard frowned. "What do you mean?"

"I mean we've been looking into your practice here. Fixing diabetes is one thing – very clever – but using a lad as a guinea pig for a new treatment without telling him. . . Not exactly ethical, is it?"

Professor Clayton thought that, along with his patient, he'd turned the corner; but his dreadful mistake was about to haunt him.

"So, unless you want me to have a little chat with the authorities, I suggest you let me speak to Wayne."

Richard sighed. Realizing that his job was on the line if this policeman carried out his threat, he nodded weakly and unwillingly.

"And there's something else."

"What?"

"I have a small device. I want you to implant it under his skin."

"You've got to be joking!"

"If you want to see Cassie O'Rourke alive, you'll do it."

"What is it?"

"Nothing that'll harm him. Just something that won't be found if he's searched."

"And what do I tell him?"

The policeman smiled and rubbed his nose. "You're very good at just getting on with a job without troubling your patient with all the details."

"Hang on. . ."

"You used his body. Unfortunately, we've got to do

something similar. Then, we call it quits and leave you alone. You get on with your life. More important, Wayne and Cassie get on with theirs. Everyone's happy."

"Two wrongs make a right, eh?" said Richard.

"I'm just doing what's best for Cassie O'Rourke."

"And if I refuse?"

"Then I'd have to raise certain matters with the medical authorities, maybe even the newspapers – things about Wayne and an actor called Arthur."

Professor Clayton closed his eyes and let out a long weary breath. "I'll go and make Wayne as comfortable as possible. But, you can't have him for long. He's too weak."

"You've got overnight to work on him. Oh, and make sure he's got those tablets for Cassie O'Rourke. I'll pick him up at dawn."

Richard shook his head in despair.

DYNAMITE 27

As soon as the intelligence officer told him that Cassie had wished him a happy birthday, O'Rourke realized his daughter was in serious trouble. He even knew that she was being threatened by a bomb. His birthday wasn't until January fourth so, by mentioning it, she was trying to tell him something. Years before, O'Rourke had agreed a secret code with his family. *One* stood for a gunman. *Two* was a petrol bomb. *Three* was a riot. *Four* was an explosive. There were several others as well. At the time, his wife and children ridiculed him, telling him he was paranoid. Yet he believed that Cassie had remembered it. By referring to his birthday – the fourth – Cassie had informed him about a bomb.

Driving through Rivelin Valley towards Ladybower Reservoir, he said in a distracted whisper, "It's nice out here, isn't it?"

The boy sitting next to him was the most sickly creature he'd ever seen, but possibly the most gutsy.

Wayne looked askance at Cassie's dad and wondered how he could talk about the scenery when he was driving towards a showdown with the terrorists who had killed his wife and sons, abducted his daughter and were bent on killing him. He might be driving to his own funeral. "Suppose."

"We're going to Strines Moor. Bleak but beautiful." In truth, O'Rourke could bear to talk only about how nice life could have been. Anything else was too painful for him. "England's got its plusses."

Annoyed by O'Rourke's calmness, Wayne snapped, "Yeah. And Northern Ireland's got its terrorists."

O'Rourke glanced at his passenger and, forced to confront the pain, asked, "Why are you helping her, Wayne?"

Wayne shrugged. "Dunno."

"Anyway, I'm grateful."

"Why here?" Wayne asked him, looking out of the window.

"Not my idea. It was Martin's. He wants to see everything that's happening for miles around. He's picked an isolated spot on the moor where he can see anyone or anything coming. No one can get close. And he didn't give the police enough time to set anything up. Their base camp is miles away, Low Bradfield. The cavalry won't be hiding behind a bush, ready to pop up and rescue us, you know. It's just you and me. Martin's planned it well, I'm afraid."

"Are you armed?" Wayne said, assuming that the car would be bristling with weapons.

"Not in the way you think."

"Uh?"

"I'm armed with the certain knowledge that fighting isn't the way forward. That's all."

Wayne shuffled his feet awkwardly. "Not even a grenade or a machine gun in the boot?"

O'Rourke shook his head and smiled faintly. "No."

The car slowed as O'Rourke applied the brake. The turning to the right, signposted for Strines Inn, was blocked by bollards. A police notice told motorists that the narrow road across the top of the desolate moor was closed.

O'Rourke got out, moved two of the bollards to one side, drew the car into the lane and stopped. "This is where I've been told to wait," he said to Wayne. "You've got something over a mile to walk. Are you sure you're up to it? And are you still sure you want to do it?"

"Yes."

"There's no shame in pulling out now, you know. You're up against a man who's as cunning as he is evil and you're going to be incredibly exposed. It's dangerous. You're injured, out of condition, and the whole thing's not your problem."

Wayne opened the door and said, "I like Cassie."

O'Rourke nodded, trying to smile. "Thanks. And good luck. Have you got her pills?"

"Yeah." Wayne set out to walk across the moor.

O'Rourke shouted, "See you soon." Then he went to move the bollards back into position.

Wayne didn't twist round. He was feeling too sore. He just raised his right arm weakly, stretching one set of stitches uncomfortably. He was a mass of bruises. The wounds that the nurses had dressed most heavily were the gashes in his abdomen and thigh. If they opened up, he could lose a lot of blood again. If he started bleeding internally again, he'd soon experience a runaway heartbeat, rapid breathing, anxiety and sweating. Exactly the symptoms he was already suffering. But Wayne guessed that, right now, his sickly condition was nothing to do with leaking blood. He was simply tired and stiff. He'd gone only two hundred metres when he started breathing deeply, needing a rest.

It was a gorgeous day, warm and sunny. The sky was broken by wisps of feathery clouds. The moor sloped gently from left to right with few undulations. Wayne could see all of the way down to Strines Reservoir. There wasn't a single tree or wall to obscure the view. No shade and no shadow. To the right of the road, a few sheep grazed but nothing else moved. No cars, no people, nothing. Wayne could imagine that he was the last person on Earth but he knew that, somewhere ahead, there were a couple of bad guys with their ailing hostage.

Normally, he would have covered a mile and a half in twenty minutes. He was a fast walker when he wanted to be. This wasn't normal, though. To give him energy, the hospital had pumped him full of carbohydrate, while his sugar police kept him in the safe zone, but his muscles were sleepy. And he ached. His head, his legs, his arms, his stomach. His skin pulled on his injuries, making them itch and smart. The sole of his left foot was somewhere between tender and excruciating. To keep himself going, he thought of that awful dead face. He was determined to save Cassie from looking like that.

Wayne screwed up his eyes against the sun's glare. The landscape to his right was punctuated with short wooden posts and wire fencing that separated the grazing fields. There was nothing that would hide terrorists. In the distance there was a square tower on a hilltop and, slightly below it, some sort of manor house but, even with binoculars, he wouldn't have got a good view of them. Topping a ridge, Wayne could see the rest of the lane winding across the moor. Between him and the distant dip where the pub must lie hidden, there was a car. It had stopped right in the middle of the road and the sight of it almost stopped Wayne's heart.

He ground to a halt, fighting to get his breath back. This far away, he couldn't see if there was anyone in the green car but he knew who would be there. Martin and the tutor would be sitting, waiting, and Cassie would be lolling in the rear. Once again, Wayne was about to tackle the boxer and the bomb-maker, the fearless combination. He inhaled the clean air, wiped his brow and trudged onward, a bloodstain appearing on his T-shirt where his stomach wound had begun to weep.

The two men got out of the car and formed a reception committee in the road. The tutor was wearing shades and holding a gun. Wayne halted about twenty paces away from them. It was like some modern-day western, a high-noon stand-off.

Martin was smiling, enjoying himself. "We were going to do this deal up on Strines Edge," he shouted, waving towards the top of the moor, "but she wouldn't have made it on foot. Looks like you're struggling as well."

Wayne did not reply.

"Let's get it over with," Martin said. "Strip off."

The security force had told Wayne that he would probably be strip-searched so he'd left his jeans behind and come in baggy trousers and boxer shorts. Even so, he was indignant and embarrassed. "What?"

"What don't you understand? Strip. Clothes off."

"Why?" asked Wayne, feigning surprise.

"Oh, come on! Even British Intelligence can dream up a plan of planting a weapon in your clothes. It doesn't take a genius. Anyway, it's not cold. Don't be shy. And Cassie's not in much of a condition to take a peek."

While Wayne struggled out of his T-shirt and trousers, Martin and the red-headed tutor walked forward. Not usually concerned about his physique, Wayne was aware of his protruding ribs and skinny arms and legs as he stood, ready for inspection, in the middle of Strines Moor.

"Fine figure of a man," Martin sneered. "Hey, your cuts have been fixed up pretty good. You couldn't have done better if you'd gone private. Someone at the Northern General must think the world of you." Martin didn't touch him at first. He just stood there, eyeing him from head to toe. "Pants as well."

Wayne turned red and looked around.

"Come on, come on."

To endure the humiliation, Wayne tried to concentrate on helping Cassie. He slipped his pants down, stepped out of them and deliberately stared into the distance, not wanting to see the bad guys' reaction. "Trainers?" he whispered, ashamed and vulnerable.

Martin completed a circle around him, looking for anything suspicious. "Let me see."

Wayne lifted up each foot in turn, staggering off balance.

Martin yanked down the socks and seemed satisfied. "No. They're normal. We'll let you keep them on. But these dressings!" Martin started feeling the cotton meticulously, prodding roughly. "You've got enough bandages to hide a rocket launcher but . . . feels like you're clean."

The tutor had been running his hands all over Wayne's clothing. He paid particular attention to the trouser pockets and plastic medicine bottle inside. "You can get dressed," he announced, thrusting the garments back at Wayne.

Relieved, Wayne slipped back into his pants as quickly as he could. Pulling his baggy trousers up over his trainers unsteadily, he spotted a cut on the right side of his waist. It was a wound he hadn't seen before. Still, he had more to worry about right now than a fresh injury adding to the many and he covered it up with his T-shirt.

"All right. Follow me. She's in the back of the car. We left the windows open because she stinks."

The sight of his once pretty girlfriend made him feel physically sick. Really, the Cassie he knew had gone. The girl in the back wasn't that first disfigured Cassie either. Spread-eagled on the seat was some brutally ravaged animal. It looked as if a rabid dog had sunk its teeth into her face. A lesion over her right eye was a window on the swirling red muscle beneath. Her skin was a mixture of reds, browns and black like autumn leaves in various states of decay. The papery stuff was falling away from under her chin revealing more twists of bloody muscle in her neck. Ugly fluids were oozing from the open sores. And she was filthy. Her hair, arms and clothes were all soiled. Her hands were behind her, probably tied.

Wayne rounded on the bad guys. "How could you?"

"She's alive," Martin stated in a matter-of-fact tone.

"She needs a hospital. I'm going to give her a pill,"

Wayne muttered, extracting the bottle from his pocket.

Martin shrugged his permission.

Wayne ducked back into the rear of the foul-smelling car and waved away several excited bluebottles. Two of them were crawling over Cassie's cheek but she didn't seem to be aware of them. She didn't feel the tablet or Wayne's hand on her blistered lips, either.

"Cassie," he said. "Open. Swallow this."

Nothing.

"It's me," he said frantically. "Wayne."

Her lips parted slightly and he forced the pill on to her swollen tongue. Then, to make sure, he gave her another. "Swallow. You must swallow."

Cassie made a muffled noise, a grunt, but she did as she was told.

Wayne hoped that she had taken the tablets properly and they were not simply lodged in her mouth or throat. It was then, when Wayne backed out of the car, that he saw the explosives sticking out from under her loose top.

"What's that?" he exclaimed, pointing.

"Dynamite," the tutor replied.

"That's. . ." Wayne ran out of words. He had forgotten how dreadful he felt, how exhausted he was, how near he was to starvation. He was consumed only with Cassie and the terrorists. "You're. . ." He gave up trying to think of words that expressed his disgust.

Martin did not react at all. He simply said, "Time for your return trip. Tell the traitor everything you've seen here. Tell him we've kept our side of the bargain. She's here and alive. Tell him we're waiting for him. When we've got him you can call in the cops – and a doctor. There's a mobile in the glove compartment."

Before he limped away, Wayne said, "Now I know why Cassie's dad had a go at you."

"You know nothing," Martin replied. "You know nothing of Ireland and Ulster."

"No, I were never any good at geography, me. But I know cruelty."

28 POISON

As soon as Wayne stumbled down from the slight ridge and came within sight of O'Rourke's car, he waved hysterically at Cassie's father, urging him to drive. Then, spent, he sank on to the verge.

When Cassie's dad dragged him to his feet and into the passenger's seat, he was streaming with sweat and tears.

"Wayne," O'Rourke cried. "What's wrong? Is she all right? Alive?"

Wayne closed his eyes in the hope of stemming the flow. "Alive, yes. All right, no. She's sick." Wayne wiped his nose with his arm, not noticing that blood had run down to his elbow. "They've got a sort of strap with dynamite on her!"

O'Rourke nodded. He wasn't surprised but he had to grit his teeth to control his emotions. "A punishment belt."

"What's she done to deserve that?" Wayne blurted out.

"She's related to me, that's what. Look, Wayne, before we go in, I've got to tell you about that sort of belt. You mustn't take it off." As best he could, O'Rourke explained about the temperature sensor that the bad guys had developed. "I suppose, if it came to it, there might be enough time for one of us to whip it off Cassie and get it against our own skin but there's no guarantee. It's very risky, very sensitive to cooling down. There'd only be a split second. They designed it so there wasn't enough time to take it off and chuck it. It'd go up before it's a metre away."

"How can you sit here so cool and talk. . ."

"Because I have to. She's my daughter. If you get an opportunity to help her, I want you to help, not blow her up. If you're going to stand a chance, I have to keep calm and tell you all about it. It's the only way. Believe me, I feel like ranting and raving – or worse – as well."

"All right."

O'Rourke gripped the steering wheel, his knuckles white, but didn't put the car in gear. "Feeling up to it?"

"No," Wayne replied.

"You can opt out any time, remember. I wouldn't blame you."

"I just wish you had an automatic rifle." To Wayne, it was stupid to walk into a vampire's lair without a sharpened wooden stake. A belief in the cross just wasn't enough.

O'Rourke attempted another smile. "Sorry."

Wayne shook his head and rubbed gently at the dressing on his thigh. "Let's get going."

His hands shaking as he held the wheel, Cassie's dad crawled along in second gear. Constantly, he peered out of the windscreen and side windows as if he were expecting a collision but there were no other vehicles on the road. Inching closer to the car that was still blocking the lane, there was no sign of Martin and the tutor. They had either ducked down out of sight in the car or behind it, or they had retreated into the field, lying flat out somewhere in the heather.

Still a hundred metres away from Cassie, O'Rourke stopped. "We don't go right up to it," he said. "The bad guys' instructions were to pull into the lay-by on the right." He pointed at the rough pull-in. "Just a minute."

He was about to get out when Wayne sat upright. "Wait! They've got a gun! They'll shoot you."

O'Rourke shook his head. "Not their style. But," he patted his chest, "just in case, it's bullet-proof."

Outside, he examined the ground closely, looking for wires or signs of disturbance. Then he got back in. "I can't see anything. It's probably OK – for the moment. But these two are good at what they do. The betting is, they've booby-trapped it. Maybe they've planted a movement detector around here somewhere."

"So, how do you know they're not about to blow us up?" Wayne asked in fright, amazed at O'Rourke's composure.

"I don't, for sure. But Martin's a talker. He's promised to tell me how to disable the punishment belt before telling me what he thinks of me and exactly why and how he's going to kill me." Gingerly, he edged forward, parked in the lay-by and turned off the ignition.

"What're you going to do about it?" asked Wayne.

"The first thing is to make sure Cassie's OK. Then I'll worry about me." He opened the door. "I'm going to see her. When I get over there, get out and move away from the lay-by. Just in case. Not too far, though."

"But how are we going to get her away?"

"If I'm not . . . capable, the key's in the ignition. You can drive, I assume. How else would you have got a conviction for driving without a licence? Head for Low Bradfield. What's that? Three or four miles away."

"But what if they blow it up?"

"Then there'll be a helicopter."

"Oh?"

"The police are listening in." O'Rourke pointed to the new wound in Wayne's side. "You're a walking microphone. It's implanted in you. They put it in you rather than me because they thought the bad guys wouldn't take any notice of another cut on you." Believing that Wayne might react badly to being used, O'Rourke added apologetically, "They told me not to tell you so you acted naturally in front of Martin. They reckoned he'd cotton on if you were conscious of it." Because he felt embarrassed, O'Rourke still didn't reveal the whole truth. Anxious to go to his daughter, he changed the subject. "Be very careful if you make a run for it with Cassie. Martin will have back-up devices around. The whole area could be mined."

Much to Wayne's surprise, when O'Rourke got out, he didn't dash towards the green car. He spread his arms, revolved once and then began to strip. Obviously, he had been given his orders before setting out and he was following them to the letter. As soon as he was naked, he turned around slowly again. Somewhere, the bad guys must be watching him, making sure that he was unarmed.

He stepped away from his clothes and headed for the other car.

Getting out on wobbly legs, Wayne watched O'Rourke lean inside the back of the car. Unable to stand, Wayne sank on to the verge again. Fiddling with the laces of his left trainer, he was wondering if O'Rourke had come to rescue his daughter or to die with her.

*

Cassie opened her eye and her mouth moved but she said nothing.

"It's all right," her dad said, stroking her hair. "It's all right. I'm here." He wiped away a tear from his own cheek and then said, "Wayne's going to get you to hospital. He's a good boy."

"But. . ." The scars down each side of her face had ruptured and were weeping poison.

"I love you, Cassie."

"But. . ."

"What is it?"

Cassie was cursing her own mouth that had become uncooperative once again. One of her hands touched the punishment belt. "A remote, Dad. He's got a remote." Every word jarred her face. She coughed and groaned with the pain. "He's going to kill us both. Now!"

O'Rourke shook his head. "I've taken care of it. There's a transmitter that's jamming their frequencies."

The phone under the dashboard rang and O'Rourke went round to the front passenger's seat to answer it.

"Very clever," Martin's voice snapped.

Understanding him at once, O'Rourke replied, "I'm not armed but it's easy to hide a miniature jammer."

Martin tutted into the phone. "Don't try anything else. Put your clothes back on. I can't stand the sight any more, traitor. Hope you've studied a map well and got your bearings. Walk due west from the car. Be precise about it. You know how we stop people wandering from the straight and narrow."

Plump flies were crawling on the side-window and

windscreen, revelling in the stench of decay. "Let the kids go, Martin," O'Rourke said. "You've got what you want. Me."

Menacingly, Martin demanded, "West. Now. If you want to know how to get Cassie's belt off."

O'Rourke dipped into the rear once more and looked at his daughter. He would have gladly taken the punishment belt from her and strapped it to himself but, if he tried it, he was likely to get them both killed. Besides, Martin would see what he had done and take gleeful revenge first on Cassie then on himself. While there was still a chance of saving Cassie, O'Rourke had to play Martin's game. He kissed her on her putrid cheek. "Got to go, love."

"No, Dad!"

"Bye, Cassie."

"No!"

He tore himself away, took a deep breath and got dressed. He'd come this far because he had no alternative. He'd come because Martin had promised to give him the instructions for removing Cassie's belt safely. But O'Rourke didn't believe he would. Really, he'd come in the hope that Martin would show mercy once he'd fulfilled his dream of eliminating the traitor. O'Rourke was offering himself in place of his daughter and, before he died, he intended to plead for her life. Crossing the road, O'Rourke began to walk into the heather, wondering whether each faltering step would be his last.

High overhead, two hang-gliders circled like hawks. The tutor tapped Martin on the shoulder and, sunlight stabbing his eyes, he pointed upwards. "There's a hang-gliding club down the road. They might not be cops."

In their freshly dug trench among the heather, Martin turned off his mobile and said, "I'm not taking any chances."

Taking a high-powered rifle, he took careful aim. A minute later, both hang-gliders were spiralling to the ground like dead pheasants, shot in mid-flight. Martin grinned. "Besides, won't do any harm to let O'Rourke see what he's up against."

Cassie's father stopped at the sound of the first gunshot and waited for the crash of the bullet entering his skull and the burning pain. But it didn't come. Instead, against a bright blue background, he watched two brave security officers plunging uselessly out of the sky.

Behind him, Cassie cried out in shock, believing that her dad had been executed.

Wayne stopped rubbing his lacerated foot, put his trainer back on, winced and made for the green car. O'Rourke had not gone far into the moorland. He was walking cautiously, his head moving from side to side as he scanned the ground for trip wires. Ducking into the car, Wayne said in a whisper, "It's OK. That weren't your dad they shot. It were two hang-gliders. How are you feeling?" He screwed up his nose against the repulsive smell.

Cassie looked no better but she seemed more aware. "Don't come near me!" Her voice was gruff and alien, gurgling through the fluids in her throat.

Taken aback, Wayne said, "Why not?"

She looked down towards the explosives at her waist.

"Don't be daft." He tried to sound unruffled but he eyed

the extravagant girdle apprehensively. "We've got to wait to see if your dad finds out how to get it off . . . you know . . . without it exploding."

Cassie shook her head tenderly.

"What's up?" asked Wayne.

"Dad's sacrificing himself. Martin's going to kill him and then me."

Wayne gazed at her for a few seconds, realizing that she wasn't being unduly pessimistic, simply realistic. "The feds and your dad'll have a plan."

Her tears diluted the very dark blood that dripped occasionally from her nose. "Hang-gliders."

"What? You think they *were* the plan? Feds parachuting in?"

She nodded so vaguely that Wayne nearly missed it.

"Fuck!" he said.

The side window had been wound down. Wayne looked out to see O'Rourke still treading carefully through the heather.

"What's happening?" Cassie spluttered.

"Dunno. Nothing." He hesitated and then said quietly, "Hang on. He's tripped up or something."

Before O'Rourke could get to his feet, Martin and the tutor leaped up from the shrubbery. This time it was Martin who had a gun in his hand. They kept O'Rourke on his knees as if he were praying before them.

Cassie was incapable of looking for herself. She expected a running commentary from Wayne.

"Er. . . He's talking to the bad guys. They're probably telling him how to get the strap off."

Cassie's eye clouded over. Even without witnessing the scene for herself, she knew what was really happening. The bad guys were carrying out a death sentence. They were teaching a lesson to everyone back home who might consider betraying them.

"Still talking."

Cassie's muscles tensed, triggering tortuous cramps.

"Can't hear what they're saying."

Gathering her remaining strength, Cassie muttered, "You go. They'll let you. They want me, not you." Unlike her, Wayne still had a life.

"Really?" Wayne asked.

"Yes."

Outside, there was a sharp crack. By the time Wayne looked across the field, all he saw was Cassie's dad falling sideways, away from the gun that Martin had held against the side of his head. "Oh, no!"

Cassie didn't have to ask. "Go," she croaked.

"Hell. They've shot him. I can't leave. . ."

"Go."

"Well. . ."

She was getting more and more animated. "Go!" This time, the order came with spit and blood.

Wayne paused, staring wide-eyed first at Martin and then at Cassie. He didn't know what to do but he admitted to himself that Cassie's words made sense. Heart and lungs on fire, he backed out of the car, hoping his legs would still support him. Before he retreated, though, he said, "Cassie?"

Cassie fixed him with the gaze from her working eye.

"You don't look so bad," he lied. "You can make it."

On the moor, the tutor was kneeling by O'Rourke's body. Wayne thought that he was attaching a wire. Perhaps he was making a booby-trap for any unwary police officers. Martin was strolling unhurriedly towards the car as if he'd got all the time in the world to complete his plan. His big shoulders swung and his red lips were curved into a smile as he closed in.

Wayne swallowed, wiped the sweat from his brow. "He's coming – probably to take the belt off."

Releasing Wayne from any obligations or guilt, Cassie replied, "Yeah. That'll be it."

"I. . ." Wayne had only seconds and words failed him. "Bye." Abandoning her, he hobbled quickly towards O'Rourke's car.

29 GUTS

The chief intelligence officer took a few seconds to make his mind up. The signals from Wayne's hidden microphone told him that O'Rourke and his airborne agents were down, probably dead, and Martin was heading towards a helpless Cassie for an unknown purpose. There was a faint chance that Martin was now satisfied and would let her go but the policeman feared the worst. He had no information on the status of the bomb-maker but he imagined that the area would be a treacherous minefield by now. He also had the complication of Wayne Wingate. If he sent in the helicopter, Martin would certainly turn on both youngsters. Letting things run their course, at least Wayne might survive. If the boy was sensible and made a dash for it, Martin would probably let him go. Besides, if he sent in the troops now, they'd be rushing into an extremely hazardous environment. There was no doubt in his mind that there would be many more casualties.

He cursed O'Rourke's decision to agree to meet Martin like this. It could have been – should have been – handled much better. With planning, with more time, the situation could have been contained. He cursed O'Rourke's emotional response to his daughter.

"No," he decided. "Keep the chopper on standby. We wait."

*

To Cassie, it seemed a long time ago that she couldn't bear to gaze on the face of a dead girl in a mirror. Sensing that Martin was standing by the car window, those same dreadful feelings came flooding back to her. She refused to open her eye because she would see not only Martin's smug expression but also her own death.

Knowing what was coming, she thought she'd be beyond panic but she wasn't. She was desperately trying to lift her feet on to the edge of the seat. She thought, if she could pass her locked hands under her backside and down to her shoes, she could thread her body through her arms. Then, with her hands at her front, she could undo the buckle and at least have the pleasure of taking Martin with her.

Her fruitless struggles made Martin laugh. Propped against the car, he pulled his baseball cap down to shield his eyes from the sunlight. Through the open window he said, "I wouldn't bother, if I were you, gorgeous. You're not well enough to be a contortionist."

Swearing under her breath, Cassie knew he was right. She was too tired, too sore, useless.

"It's a good day. A day that marks the end of the line for the O'Rourkes, the end of the line for all traitors."

Recognizing the hopelessness of her situation, Cassie spluttered, "Get on with it."

"You don't mind if I stay out here, do you? It's more palatable in the fresh air." Not getting a response, Martin said, "Bottle and intelligence. You even know why I'm going to kill you, don't you?"

"Yes."

Martin smiled. "I could just let your face poison you – it's doing a pretty good job – but I don't want headlines about natural causes or medical mistakes. That wouldn't suit at all. For my purpose – teaching everyone back home not to mess with the IFG – it has to be clear-cut. It doesn't get more clear-cut than a bullet, does it? But I promised you, I'd do it quickly. It'll be painless as well – not like a transplant going pear-shaped. You deserve that."

Cassie took a last miserable breath.

Martin placed the revolver against the cleft down the side of her head, an open door for the bullet.

Before he could pull the trigger, Martin turned in total astonishment. Almost silently, O'Rourke's car was nearly upon him. That brat, Wayne Wingate, had released the handbrake and was steering the car straight at him! It should have blown up as soon as it began to roll. O'Rourke's electronic device must have jammed the radio signal from the movement detector hidden beside the lay-by. Damn both of them, O'Rourke and Wingate!

Martin swung round with the gun and fired twice at the windscreen on the driver's side. The glass shattered but he saw no one inside.

He flattened himself against the door, realizing that the runaway car would just scrape him. Yet the emerging smile on his face did not last for long. The front wheel ran over his right foot and he cried out. Resisting the temptation to clutch his throbbing foot, he kept his mind on the job. He had waited a long time for this moment and he would not let pain distract him from the culmination of his plans. Once more, he readied himself for the final execution.

As soon as the car slid past, Martin was taken by surprise again. Wayne leaped out from behind it, metal glinting in his hand.

Wayne had taken only one precaution. Before he left the hospital he had liberated Professor Clayton's scalpel. Knowing that the bad guys were likely to examine his clothes and body, he could think only of putting it in his trainer and hoping for the best. When he'd wrapped up the blade to protect his sole from its sharpness, he'd not been able to squeeze his foot in as well. Instead, he'd slipped it in uncovered and put up with it ripping his flesh like a vicious nail through the tread of his shoes. When Martin had told him to strip, he'd volunteered to remove his trainers in a show of audacity. The bluff had worked. Martin had lost interest in his footwear. Now, Wayne pushed hard against the car's boot and, when it began to move, he crouched behind with the scalpel in his hand.

He imagined that it would be very hard to kill a man. He imagined that his sense of right and wrong would have stopped him. But it was easy to make an exception for Martin. From behind the car, Wayne dived at the terrorist. He didn't aim at a particular part of the bad guy's body. He wasn't that calculating. He just went for his middle and jabbed as hard as he could.

He felt Martin's taut belly, horrible warm liquid and something spongy. He saw his hand turn completely red. He heard Martin's howl and the gun falling to the ground. Amazing himself, horrifying himself, he stabbed Martin again – this time in the chest, driving a stake into the cold heart of the vampire – and kicked the gun away, into the grass border.

Martin's squeal dwindled to a sigh and then to silence.

Wayne wasn't a violent, vindictive boy. He stood there, unable to take in what he had done. He knew only that he'd not acted for himself. If he'd been thinking solely about himself, he would have walked away by now. If he'd been fit, he would have sprinted like he used to run away from supermarkets with stolen chocolate in his hand. No, not this time. He'd faced up to Martin for what he'd done to Cassie, her family and other people like them.

"What's. . .?" Hearing Cassie's weak voice, Wayne looked up from the sprawling inhuman shape on the ground.

O'Rourke's car had trundled down the lane and come to a halt on the verge, lodged against a wire fence. Movement did catch Wayne's eye, though. It was the tutor. He'd begun to make for them but, almost at once, he stopped, turned and went off in the opposite direction, towards Derwent Edge.

Wayne stepped over the immobile body and clambered in beside Cassie. "Right. Time to sort you out."

"No! You've. . ."

"Do you want to get blown up?"

"You should've gone. . . The belt. . ."

"Cassie?"

"Yes?"

"Shut up!"

Wayne's brain might be slow but he had an idea. He went to the front seat and fiddled under the dashboard until he found the bonnet release. He pulled it, dashed to the front of the car and lifted the hood. Putting his hand against the grimy engine, he nodded. It was still warm.

Opening the back door on the other side, away from Martin, Wayne said to Cassie, "You've got to help me. I need you leaning against the front of the car, like."

"What?"

"Come on," he said, grabbing hold of her and easing her out. "I'll show you."

Cassie could hardly move. She managed to push a little with her legs but otherwise, she just flopped. She certainly couldn't stand so it was up to Wayne. Running on empty, Wayne yanked Cassie out of the seat and pressed her against the side of the car to keep her upright. In the sunshine, her face was even more shocking but Wayne had to ignore it. He grabbed her around the shoulders as if he were helping a drunk to take a few paces towards a bed. He avoided touching the hideous thing at her midriff.

Dragging her to the front of the car, he propped her against the wing.

Gasping for breath, he said, "Right. I'm going to take the belt off and leave it on the engine. It's still hot enough, I reckon. Hotter than you."

"No."

"Yes," he insisted. "I'm going to push you up so you're lying across. . ."

"You'll kill us."

"We can't wait for help. The tutor could detonate it any time."

Cassie was crying again. She didn't want this. None of it. She didn't want to risk Wayne. She didn't want to risk herself. She just wanted what she couldn't have: a normal, safe life. But Wayne had a point. With the punishment belt around her waist, she'd be easy meat for the tutor. Neither she nor Wayne knew that the device implanted in Wayne's side was jamming radio signals from the remote control. "All right," she muttered, so quietly that her reluctant consent was almost inaudible.

Squatting down by her knees, Wayne said, "Just watch yourself. When I push up, you save yourself from bashing your head against the engine. Go down on a shoulder or something."

Cassie sighed in resignation.

Wayne steeled himself, began to tug and fell over. His head was pounding, fresh blood had soaked into the bandage around his thigh and was dribbling down his leg. He got up and tried again, heaving on Cassie's knees until she slid up the wing and fell across the warm engine. She went down with a thump like a joint of meat dropped on to a kitchen work surface.

"Are you all right?" he asked in panic.

"Uh."

Wayne took her groan as a good sign. "Right." He lifted up her T-shirt and examined the punishment belt. The sight of the thing made him break out into another sweat and his heart hammered in his chest yet again. He couldn't believe he was doing this. He'd got to the age of sixteen without confronting anything. He'd always turned the other cheek. Yet, if he was going to reach seventeen with Cassie, he had to confront this bomb.

There was a fancy-looking buckle at the front. It wasn't

216

ornate, just complicated. A small wire led from it to the detonator at Cassie's side. At once, Wayne realized that the temperature sensor was behind the buckle, pressed against Cassie's feverish skin. Touching her, Wayne felt a wave of pity. She was burning up. It was a wonder that she hadn't melted the sensor. Now, he just had to hope he could undo the buckle and press it on to the engine block quickly enough. He couldn't fumble or hesitate or drop it or put it on to a cool part of the car. It had to nestle against the block near the spark plugs. That's where most of the heat remained. If he made a mistake, he'd never make another.

He manhandled Cassie, rolling her to one side so that the belt came as close as possible to the engine but wasn't trapped under the weight of her body. He had to hope that her high temperature would give him a few more fractions of a second before the sensor cooled to its trigger point and set off an explosion that would rip Cassie apart and take him with her.

His voice sounded like someone else's. It was unsteady and high-pitched. "I'm going to do it, all right?"

Cassie did not respond.

"If I get it off OK, I want you to help. We'll have to get away from here. Can you do that?"

Cassie issued a grunt that could have meant anything.

"Here we go."

Wayne could hardly control his hands. They were shaking and his palms were wet with oil, sweat and blood. He shivered when he touched the metal clasp, as if he'd just come into contact with a poisonous snake. He withdrew his fingers, took a deep breath and started again. The top plate was hinged on one side. Clearly, he had to pull it up to unfasten it. He slipped two fingernails under the lip and, for the first time in his life, felt like saying a prayer. He glanced up at Cassie's wounded face. Her eyelids were closed and he wondered if she was praying.

He couldn't delay any more. He gripped the belt with his left hand and levered up the plate with the tensed fingertips of his right. He felt the belt slacken slightly as the clasp flew open but he kept the buckle and, he hoped, the sensor pressed down on Cassie's bare and burning skin.

As far as he could tell, the belt was now unattached and only the pressure of his quivering hand kept it in place. With his right hand he unthreaded the free end of the belt from around Cassie's waist. The buckle was swimming in warm sweat from Cassie's midriff and his own palm, the sticks of dynamite lying dormant by her stomach.

"It's undone," he whispered as if sound could set it off. He swallowed hard and said, "I'm going to take it off now."

Bracing himself for the bang, Wayne lifted the buckle a couple of centimetres from her skin and instantly slid his hand underneath. The sensor was now against his own palm. "Go. You can go," he whispered urgently.

Cassie fidgeted but was incapable of levering herself up from the engine. Even if her hands hadn't been tied behind her back, she would have been powerless to escape.

Clutching the strap with his left hand, Wayne placed his right up against the engine block. Holding his breath, he yanked his right hand away and immediately pressed the buckle on to the hot metal. Supporting the rest of the belt on the wires that led to the spark plugs, Wayne gingerly moved his hands away.

"Done!" he almost shouted. Not thinking of his own frailty, he grasped Cassie's upper arms and hauled her back on to her feet. "Let's go!"

He didn't know which way was safe but the other car had rolled down the lane without setting off any mines so Wayne headed in the same direction, dragging a barely conscious Cassie with him. He was so intent on not dropping her that he failed to hear the throbbing of helicopter blades.

Stumbling, both Wayne and Cassie fell behind her father's car and passed out, Wayne's arms still encircling her protectively.

Neither of them saw the punishment belt fall from the engine. Before it hit the road underneath, it exploded in a thunderous blast. The green car leaped into the air and immediately burst into flame. Sheltered behind O'Rourke's car, Cassie and Wayne did not feel the heat. The shower of glass and shrapnel passed them by.

They were not even aware of being air-lifted to hospital.

The tutor did not dare to go back to help Martin. He did not dare to walk on the heath that he'd Semtexed liberally. At heart he was a coward. He was paid to blow things up, not to risk his life.

With Martin, he had planned a couple of options to get away. There was always the car. They hadn't fixed it to detonate in case they needed it. But the punishment belt would have blown it up anyway because, by now, they'd expected Cassie's dead body to be cooling. Anyway, there was always the risk of running into police roadblocks with that car. The second plan, and the one that the tutor chose, was the scenic route. Cursing Cassie, Wayne and the fierce sun, he sprinted along the footpath where no police cars could chase him, past Black Tor, lurching down the steep path into Derwent Valley to emerge between Ladybower and Derwent Reservoirs. There, he had parked a second car with a change of clothing in the boot.

CANCER 30

Without warning, Cassie sat up in her bed and said, "What's that?"

"What?"

"That noise."

Back in a private room of the Department of Experimental Medicine, Wayne listened for a few moments. "What noise? I can't hear anything."

"It was a clicking," said Cassie. "Or maybe a tick."

"Probably one of the greys outside with a walking stick," Wayne replied with a grin.

Since the death of her father on Strines Moor two weeks before, Cassie's nerves had been shot to pieces. Cars, belts and moors had been added to her list of phobias. Even Wayne reminded her of events she'd rather forget. Earlier in the day, she had brought the ward to a complete halt by insisting that she'd seen Martin pouring petrol over a patient when it was only a nurse giving a bed-bath to a cancer victim whose skin had been made temporarily transparent ready for surgery. He was the one who made the model aeroplanes.

The nurses had told Wayne that it would be a long time before they could rebuild Cassie's life. Eventually, she would regain her confidence but there would always be psychological damage. He could not expect miracles.

Buoyed by little green pills, though, her face was nearly mended. No miracles there, either. Cassie had been left with permanent blemishes. They weren't ugly. They were discoloured patches. And Wayne preferred her with them. Somehow, they seemed right on a girl who'd been through hell, like shiners on a boxer after a long hard contest. Perfect healing would have made a mockery of her suffering.

"No one can get in," Wayne reassured her. "Combination lock."

"You did."

Wayne smiled and held up his hands. "Magic fingers, remember."

As for Wayne, he too had been left with scars after his various wounds had healed, but emotional trauma had not been able to penetrate his thick skin. His diabetic body had been brought back under control by the robotic sugar police surfing his bloodstream. All of the other nanorobots had been purged from him – after all, he'd only just survived himself so they didn't stand a chance. There were no other secret machines inside him. Professor Clayton had removed the transmitter in his side and returned it to the security force.

The hospital was desperate to discharge him and free up a bed. Social Services had been in to talk about placing him with foster parents or reuniting him with his uncle and aunt or finding him a place in a home. It would take longer before Cassie could also leave, with a supply of anti-rejection tablets, frequent check-ups, repeat prescriptions, and regular counselling.

Wayne was trying his best to distract her. "RoboBoy, me,"

he said happily. "Anyone got something to test, they stick it in me first."

Cassie heard him but she didn't react straightaway. She was still listening for the imaginary ticking as if she suspected a bomb had been concealed in the room. After a few seconds, she perked up. Going through physiotherapy for a second time, she was mastering the art of smiling again. "You should let someone else volunteer for a change."

Wayne shook his head. "No chance." He had got used to being the centre of attention, to being important. He enjoyed it when medics made a fuss over him. Suddenly miserable, he added, "They're making me go home – as soon as I get one to go to."

"That's good."

"But. . ."

"What?"

Wayne looked embarrassed. "I'd . . . like . . . have to leave you."

Cassie shrugged as if it were a foregone conclusion that no one would want to be with a complete wreck. "What about the Hillsborough house?"

Wayne nodded. "I asked if we could have it."

"We?"

"Yes, but everything's changed now."

"Is it?"

Wayne nodded. "They're not doing any . . . what-do-you-call-it any more. Cosmetic stuff on greys. They're just curing diseases and disfigurements, so they don't want us as adverts."

Cassie sighed distractedly. "We're not supermodels any more. Oh, well."

"We're the same, you and me."

"Are we?" Her face crinkled. "How do you make that out?"

As always, Wayne thought about what he was going to say only after he'd reached the point of no return. "Well, you know. Both abandoned in hospital, not a mum or a dad between us."

Cassie's head drooped. She realized that he was trying to make her feel better, less alone and resentful, but his counselling skills were off the bottom of the scale. If he'd hoped his remark would draw them together, he had failed spectacularly. She retreated into a world inhabited by her mum, dad and her brothers.

Hilary Staunton no longer had a young picturesque advertisement. Her first human subject had been spoiled. Her fifth, Dorothy Heywood, was dead. Yet Hilary didn't blame herself and she didn't feel any remorse for what she'd done. The damage done was down to everyone else. She was simply rebuilding lives the best way she knew. With single-minded determination. Along the way, there were bound to be failures.

The university had held a hasty investigation into the activities of the Department of Experimental Medicine and decided to put a ban on cosmetic treatments. For all of his pious words, that was Richard Clayton's fault because he'd brought the unit into disrepute by being far less ethical than she was herself.

Dorothy Heywood's unsatisfactory treatment was the fault of her own body chemistry. For the future, Hilary would work out a test so she could check patients for the same rare and violent reaction to the anti-rejection drug before she performed a transplant.

Cassie O'Rourke's problems were the fault of Irish politics, her father and some grubby extremist called Martin. Like Hilary, this Martin had pursued his own goals with single-minded determination, trusting that the end justified the means. He'd believed that, to rebuild life in Northern Ireland, he had to destroy first. Along the way, there were bound to be victims.

Professor Staunton had a duty to continue her work on transplants, insisting that repairing severely disfigured faces should not be called cosmetic. She agreed to the university's new policy but, to give herself a safety net, she also took a part-time post at a private clinic where she was beyond the university's ban.

When it happened, it all fell into place incredibly quickly. Within a few days, Wayne was perched on Cassie's bed, feeling torn. Sitting in an easy chair, looking worn yet attractive, Cassie was half-listening to him.

"I've got a place in some care home up in Shirecliffe," Wayne announced.

"Oh?"

"They took me there yesterday."

"Is it nice?"

"Suppose."

"What about the people?"

Wayne shrugged. "Dunno. OK, I guess." He didn't sound enthusiastic because he would have preferred to stay close to Cassie. He would have preferred to stay where he was, strutting around the cheerfully decorated ward, healthier than anyone else again. He managed to sound more eager when he added, "I could work on them. See if they've got a place for you as well. You know, when you're ready."

Cassie shook her head. "I don't know what's going to happen to me." She sounded indifferent to her future.

Deciding to risk it, Wayne stood up, leaned towards her and kissed her. Her lips scarcely responded, though. She seemed caught between surprise and indifference.

"When are you going?" she asked.

"Now."

Cassie nodded. "I see."

Wayne was hurt. He expected more from her.

Never before had he wondered where life was taking him. He just went with the flow. Now, he saw two paths opening up for him. He saw a choice. One way was the world, the other was Cassie's claustrophobic, precarious life. One way had infinite possibilities, the other forced him to be carer and companion before he had a hope of being a boyfriend. One way required no effort, the other would be hard work.

Wayne took a deep breath. "Bye, then."

"Yeah. And . . . thanks."

Wayne paused and added, "I've got to come in for check-ups, like. Maybe I'll visit you."

"OK. That'd be good."

At the door, Wayne said, "Cassie. I. . ."

"What?"

"Nothing. Bye." He walked away without the swing in his shoulders.

"But I did!" Cassie cried.

The counsellor looked at her with a mixture of sympathy, compassion and detachment. "You've got to ask yourself, Cassie, is it likely? The police'll be looking for him so he's not going to turn up here."

"Here's the last place they'll look."

"All right. But how's he going to get in? He was a tutor, wasn't he, not a doctor or a nurse?"

"No, I mean he's a patient. I saw him! Really. On the ward."

The counsellor shook her head. "He's not going to be able to feign an illness, Cassie. Maybe people can fake it in A and E – until they see a doctor – but not here. It's only genuine cases that get this far. Honest. You're safe. I don't really want to prescribe more tranquillizers."

"But he's in one of the other private rooms. I know he is!" she said defiantly.

"You've got to expect a little confusion still," the psychologist replied. "You saw someone who looked a bit like him, that's all. Remember, you thought you saw Martin in the ward and he's dead. The brain plays funny tricks after a shock."

Cassie had to admit, she'd seen her mum and dad, her brothers, Bernie. But that was different. She knew she was deluding herself with them. She'd brought them back in her head for company. The tutor was flesh and blood. "He had a funny neck."

There was a knock at the door before it opened. "Ah," the counsellor said, "the one who's not supposed to know the code, but does. Come in. I'm just off anyway. You talk to Cassie."

As soon as the medic left, Cassie carried on as if Wayne had never been away. "He's here! I saw him." She was almost hysterical.

Expecting some sort of welcome and having rehearsed his own greeting, Wayne felt peeved. "Who?" he asked tersely.

"The tutor."

"What? No chance."

"No one believes me!" Cassie uttered in frustration. Her fist hit the mattress.

Wayne did not have to ask her if she was better. Plainly, she was still upset and volatile. He didn't believe that the tutor would turn up at the hospital but he wondered if he could calm Cassie down by humouring her. "I'll take a look around if you like," he said.

"No!"

"Why not?"

"It's too dangerous. What if he sees you?"

"I'll be careful, me," Wayne replied, heading for the door. "Whereabouts was he?"

"Oh, all right," she said, grateful for his persistence. "I was going to the bathroom. They were taking him into the next but one private room. The skin on his neck and shoulder was transparent. Horrible."

Wayne was relieved that the hospital hadn't changed the code as he tapped in 1987. He turned the handle of the third side-door on the left, opened it a few centimetres and peered inside. The light was off so he couldn't see much. There was an inert lump in the bed, though.

Just as Wayne was about to tiptoe into the room, he was yanked out by a nurse. "Can't you keep your nose out of anything, Wayne Wingate? You were trouble enough when you were a patient. Now you're making yourself a nuisance even when you're not."

Wayne could tell by her wry smile that she wasn't entirely serious. He kept the door open very slightly by wedging it with his foot. "I were just. . ."

She looked at her watch and said, "Your appointment's in five minutes."

"Who's in here?" Wayne asked quietly, pointing into the room.

"That's an impertinent question, young man."

"I mean, what's he got? I'm just trying to sort something out for Cassie, trying to put her mind at rest."

The nurse seemed more understanding at the mention of Cassie O'Rourke. "If you must know, the poor man's got skin cancer."

"Skin cancer?" Wayne murmured thoughtfully, almost to himself.

"Yes. Why?"

Wayne glanced in horror at the dark chink between the door and the frame. "Red hair, pale skin, sunburned?"

The nurse nodded. "If you've got pale skin, you've got to be careful in the sun these days, even though we've got a new way. . ."

Increasingly concerned, Wayne interrupted in a hushed voice. "Is that where you make the skin see-through?"

"Yes. That's how the professor gets a good look at the melanoma – the tumours."

"What's he doing now?"

"Who?" asked the nurse.

Wayne inclined his head towards the door. "The bloke with cancer."

Behind them, a musician began to play a chirpy clarinet.

"Are you sure this is for Cassie?"

Wayne nodded.

Seeing his serious expression, the nurse did not doubt his word. "He's gone off for tests. A scan. He needs urgent treatment."

"So, who's in his bed?"

The nurse looked puzzled.

"Yes. There's someone in his bed."

She took a peep inside and then replied, "He must have come back already. Probably tired. He's taking a nap."

Moving away from the door and letting it close, Wayne whispered, "Cassie thinks he's a mad bomber."

"She's very imaginative at the moment. Disturbed."

"Yeah, but what if she's right?"

Another nurse, telephone gripped between her shoulder and neck, shouted, "I've got Radiography on the line here, wanting to know where their patient is. He hasn't turned up."

The nurse standing next to Wayne exchanged a worried frown with him before replying, "He left quarter of an hour ago. I watched him go."

"Well, he's not in Radiography."

Wayne said, "If Cassie's right. . ." He glanced fearfully at the closed door as if it too had become transparent and he could see the hump in the bed.

"No," the nurse said. "No one in their right minds. . . Not in a hospital."

"If he wants to blow Cassie up, he's not going to do it when he's around himself, is he? Maybe he's gone and left behind—"

"You're jumping the gun," she answered, interrupting as if she didn't want to hear what Wayne was about to say. "We don't even know if it's the same man, whether he got lost, came back and fell asleep, or whatever." She began to punch the code into the security lock.

"Suppose. But what if it is him? Don't go in. He might have booby-trapped it."

The nurse hesitated. "I'll call for one of the professors."

"Good with bombs, are they?"

She glanced at Wayne with a harsh expression, wondering what else he expected her to do.

Left alone by the door, watching two frail greys across the way clapping in time to the clarinet, Wayne had a terrifying thought. What if it was a bomb and what if it was on some sort of fuse or timer? Every second of delay reduced the chances of evacuating the patients. Wayne had always had zero tolerance towards greys but they didn't deserve to be blasted out of their beds. And then there was Cassie, the real target. Or was it Wayne himself? If the tutor had got himself admitted for skin cancer, it wouldn't have been beyond his wit to sneak a look in the appointments book. He might have known that Wayne would be having his check-up this morning.

It was then that the nurse's words echoed in his head. "Your appointment's in five minutes."

Five minutes! At once, Wayne understood. He was sure there was a bomb in the room and it would be set to go off in five minutes when he was due in the department. After all, he was the one who'd wrecked the bad guys' plans. The tutor was nailing them both at the same time. At least if the bomb was rigged to detonate at a certain time, it wouldn't explode when someone switched the light on or pulled back the sheets. But Wayne didn't know which way to turn. He wanted to go and warn Cassie, to get her out of the ward, yet he didn't have a scrap of evidence that they were in danger. He might just be getting carried along with her fantasy. Really, there was only one sensible thing to do. If he was going to avoid making a fool of himself, he needed proof.

He took a deep breath and, once again, tapped out the combination. This time, his fingers were trembling.

PLASTIC 31

Wayne hesitated before he switched the light on. For a moment, he wondered if it would be the last thing he ever did but he was convinced that, if there was an explosive in the private room, it would be a time bomb.

The strip light flickered and then settled to a bright line bisecting the ceiling. Wayne walked gingerly towards the bed, his heart racing. It wasn't like the time when he'd unveiled that woman's dead face, though. Now, it was plain that the lump under the sheet was the wrong shape to be a human being. It looked like five or six pillows collected in the middle of the bed. Slowly, Wayne tiptoed towards it. He seemed to be on the point of bursting till he realized that he was holding his breath. He let out a long rush of air.

He gasped and nearly leaped out of his skin when the door behind him opened. He spun round and there was Cassie. He wanted to tell her to run away, to make her bid for safety, but he was so pleased to see her that he didn't even try. He was relieved to have her with him. Besides, she was wearing a gritty look, intent on showing the world that she was right. Together they approached the ominous bulge in the bedding without a word.

Wayne went round one side of the bed and Cassie stayed on the other. Standing opposite each other, they exchanged nervous glances. Swallowing hard, Wayne whispered, "We'd better have a look and see what's underneath, what we're up against."

Unsteadily, Cassie bent down and grasped her side of the sheet with quivering hands. Both Cassie and Wayne took a deep breath and then lifted up the sheet and pulled it back gingerly. Cassie screamed aloud. Wayne screamed on the inside, soundlessly.

They were looking at a huge slab of plastic explosive, packed around a detonator.

Cassie was rooted to the spot. "My God!"

Aghast, Wayne moved round the bed towards Cassie but he stopped at the foot. Attached to the stuff that looked like grey plasticine was a clock. It had just gone past 10.58. Its minute hand was inching uncompromisingly towards eleven o'clock, the time of Wayne's appointment. The pointer that ticked away the seconds jerked in sixty small steps around the clock face. Beside the clock was a dial showing 11.05 and a countdown: six minutes and twenty seconds.

His whole body tingling unbearably, Wayne nodded. By setting the bomb to go off at five past eleven, the tutor had allowed Wayne five minutes in case he turned up late for his check-up.

Cassie's pulse drummed ferociously. Joining Wayne, she stared at the seconds ticking away, far too quickly. "What do we do?" she stammered.

His natural inclination was to run like crazy. In six minutes, he'd be able to get a safe distance away with Cassie.

"Well?" she cried. "We can't just make a run for it."

"Suppose not," Wayne replied. It would take two nurses

six minutes just to get one decrepit patient out of a bed and into a wheelchair. A lot of the greys looked as if they didn't have long to live anyway but the tutor shouldn't be the one to call time on them. That should be down to the medics, the gods and themselves.

"Stop the clock," Cassie whispered. "That's what we do."

"No. I bet, if we took the batteries out or snipped a wire, it'd go up anyway. He'll have booby-trapped it, like. That's what happens in films anyhow."

The door flew open and Hilary Staunton appeared. "What's. . .?" Her eyes shifted to the bed and she uttered, "Bloody hell!"

Wayne and Cassie both stepped back, clearing the way for a responsible adult to take charge. Wayne waved his hand towards the timer mechanism. "We've got six . . . less than six minutes."

Professor Staunton's impressive list of qualifications meant nothing. She was at a complete loss. The colour drained from her cheeks and she muttered, "Don't look at me."

But Wayne and Cassie *were* gaping at her, waiting.

"I'll go and phone the police, the bomb squad. And evacuate the ward." With an expression that was a mixture of shock, distress and embarrassment, she disappeared as suddenly as she'd come.

Wayne stared at Cassie and shook his head frantically. "Not a hope. Five minutes. No one'll be here in five minutes. And she won't clear the ward either."

"We're on our own," Cassie gasped.

Wayne was used to being let down by adults. "We've got

to stop the clock without cutting the current. But I don't know how."

Cassie hesitated for a moment and then, shaking off her terror, she dashed out of the room. "Just a minute."

Wayne closed his eyes and sighed. One minute, yes. That would be all right. But five minutes would be too late. He felt as if he'd been locked in a cage with a hungry lion. When he knelt down warily to get a closer look at the back of the clock, he could have been putting his head in the lion's mouth.

Cassie ran out into the ward, past the oblivious clarinet player who was still chirruping jovial tunes, and up to the reception desk. A nurse, panicking into the phone, was astounded by Cassie's burst of energy.

"It *is* a bomb!" Cassie shrieked. "A time bomb. Professor Staunton's seen it. We've got five minutes."

"I know," the nurse replied. "Hilary's. . ." She waved a hand towards the other end of the ward. "But it's nowhere near enough. . ."

"Plaster!" Cassie exclaimed, interrupting. "The stuff you fix broken arms with. We need it."

The nurse looked blankly at her. "What? We don't keep any on this ward. You'd have to. . ."

Cassie didn't linger to find out what she'd have to do. Instead, she glanced around the ward. She'd never seen so many staff at the same time. Several doctors and nurses were trying to assess which patients could be moved quickly, which would stand a chance. Staring at the old cancer patient who'd surrounded himself with model aircraft and whose neck was no longer transparent, Cassie muttered, "Yes!" She darted towards him and, without a word of explanation, rummaged among the kit on his table. Scattering model-making tools and patiently constructed aeroplane parts, she snatched what she wanted.

The old man just sat there in bed, lost for words, gaping. He could manage only a grunt, "Oi!"

Cassie ignored him, ran up to the private room and again keyed the code, 1987. Inside, on his knees, Wayne seemed to be praying beside the bomb. The countdown was displaying 2.44. "Here you go," she said breathlessly, thrusting the tube at him.

"What's this?"

"Glue."

"So?"

"You're down there. You do it."

"What?"

"Squeeze it into the clock and gum up the works."

Wayne thought about it for a few seconds.

"Get on with it!" Cassie cried. "Or shift yourself so I can do it myself."

"No. I'll give it a go." He took the tube from her, saying, "It's not a digital clock so it'll have cogs and things. Glue might just clog it up."

"Hurry up." Goading him, Cassie said, "Two minutes left."

"I can see that."

A couple of knobs protruded through holes in the back of the clock. Quickly, Wayne unscrewed the lid from the tube of glue and, very gently, placed its tip alongside the upper knob as close as possible to the narrow hole. Holding his breath again, he squeezed. Releasing its fruity smell, some of the clear fluid ballooned sideways but Wayne thought that some had gone inside. To make sure, he squeezed again, emptying half of the tube's contents into the top hole.

Still squatting, he leaned back and, with Cassie, waited. One minute forty seconds, one minute thirty seconds, one minute twenty seconds. The juddering hand rotated relentlessly and obstinately like a shark encircling its prey before pouncing.

"It's not going to stop," Wayne murmured. He could feel his hair standing on end.

"Put more in."

Wayne nodded and gulped at the same time.

"Go on, then! Or let me in."

"It's not that." Wayne hated the thought of putting his head down so close to the explosive again. He didn't want to think about what would happen if the bomb went up, but his imagination provided a gruesome picture. Of course, if the explosion came, he wouldn't know much about it. Forcing himself, he leaned over the dreadful device again and tackled the second hole this time. There didn't seem to be much point in doing it bit by bit so he squeezed the entire contents of the tube into the lower opening. Some of the glue bulged outwards forming a clear tacky collar around the knurled knob but much of it must have squirmed inside.

The number of minutes had disappeared from the display. Their remaining time was measured in meagre seconds. Fifty-seven, fifty-six, fifty-five. . .

Wayne scrambled to his feet and stood back. "It's not going to work," he muttered to himself but aloud. An unpleasant quiver enveloped his whole body as he realized that he was inside the final minute of his life. Every muscle in his body tensed and seemed to pull on his heart.

Forty-eight, forty-seven. . .

"It is," replied Cassie, trying to sound as if she meant it. "The glue needs time to set." For once she found within herself a need to pray. She looked up at the ceiling and pleaded, "Please. We really don't deserve this."

Forty, thirty-nine, thirty-eight. . .

Wayne jolted in surprise when something gripped his arm firmly. Looking down, he saw that it was Cassie's taut hand. He turned towards her, clasped her in a hug and wept on to her shoulder. "You're so good," he mumbled. Wishing that an embrace could protect her – protect them both – from the blast, he said, "I'm sorry. . ."

Thirty-one, thirty. . .

Cassie shrank back from him a little. Freeing one hand she waved towards her marked face and asked, "You really wouldn't have minded this?"

Ashamed that she was seeing him cry, he hid himself in another hug. "Of course not," he said into her ear.

Twenty-one, twenty, nineteen. . .

Unable to tear her eye away from the countdown, Cassie watched the vile thing from over his shoulder. "Wayne?" Her voice fell between a question and an exclamation.

"What?"

Faltering but not with fear and dread this time, she said,

"I think. . . Look." She pulled away from him and jabbed a finger towards the clock. "It is! Look. It's slowing down."

Wayne wiped his eyes. "No, it's. . . Yes, it's happening!" Cassie's idea was beginning to work.

Fourteen. . . Thirteen. . . Twelve. . .

The clock hand struggled to finish its circuit of the face, trying desperately to drag itself up to the vertical. It was taking much longer than a second to complete each tick but it was determined to reach the summit.

Eleven. . . Ten. . .

Cassie clasped her hands together and glanced upwards. "Thank you, thank you."

But the clock had not yet given up the fight against the stiffening glue.

Wayne warned her, "It might still. . ."

Nine. . .

Eight. . .

And there it stopped.

After a full minute the pointer had not moved and Cassie could breathe again. "We've done it!" she cried. "It's bunged up. I just know it is." She threw herself into Wayne's arms.

TEARS 32

The funeral had been delayed until Cassie was well enough to cope with it. Hardly anyone else had turned up for the service, though. The men that O'Rourke mixed with most were in the security force and it was too risky for them to show up in public. His friends, unaware of his new identity and his fate, were back in Northern Ireland. The priest talked about the benefits of slipping away quietly and simply in a homely atmosphere but Cassie didn't believe him. Back in Dublin, lots of people had turned out to bury Martin. Four men in balaclavas fired guns over his coffin in a military tribute. It had even been on the news. There were no tributes for a man who died for peace, no TV cameras, only Cassie's tears and Wayne's respect.

Afterwards, Cassie sat on a wooden bench in the leafy crematorium while her social worker waited patiently in a car parked down the lane. "You know," she said quietly, "Dad would've liked it here."

They were well within the city boundary but the grounds were peaceful and rustic. The garden was dotted with trees, shrubs and roses. In the pond on their left, huge koi carp glided serenely while water trickled down from a marble statue of a naked child. Visitors spoke in hushed voices or walked silently among the flower beds. Sunlight streamed down, taking away any suggestion of gloominess.

"Suppose. He said he liked the countryside when we were . . . you know . . . on the moor."

Cassie nodded and gripped the arm of the bench harder.

"At least it's all over now," Wayne said, trying to reassure her.

"Yeah."

The security officers had consulted the Department of Experimental Medicine and learned that the tutor was dying. Their counterparts in Dublin had arrested him when he registered for treatment in a private hospital. Now, he would get his therapy only under armed guard. At best, medicine would probably give him another few months of life. He was unlikely ever to see a courtroom, a judge, a guilty verdict and a sentence. His punishment would take a different form.

Wayne stood up, expecting that Cassie would follow suit, but she remained seated.

"Are you off?" she asked.

"Suppose," said Wayne, not able to hide the disappointment in his face.

"I guess we've seen a lot together, you and me, but. . ." Cassie sighed. "You've got that home to go to, I'm getting a foster family. Parting of the ways."

"Is it?"

Cassie would have liked to face the future with Wayne but he was a living, painful reminder. Every time she looked at him, heard him, touched him, she remembered the torment. It came rushing back into her mind and overwhelmed her. The counsellor had assured her that, with time and distance, she'd beat the feelings of dread. But, attached to Wayne, she would never get the distance she needed. Besides, she couldn't believe that Wayne would willingly put up with her bruised spirit and battered body. "Bye, Wayne."

Wayne lingered for a few seconds, his face downcast, his shoulders slumped, before he muttered something and sauntered away.

He shuffled over the little wooden bridge above the ornamental pond and had begun to walk disconsolately across the decking when he heard her call his name softly. At once, he perked up, stopped and turned round.

Cassie was leaning on the handrail at the other end of the convex bridge. "Did you mean what you said?"

"What?" he said from his side of the decorative bridge.

"You really don't mind my face."

"Yes, of course I meant it. You look good to me. Right good."

"But you couldn't look me in the eye and say it."

Wayne looked round to make sure no one could overhear. "I didn't want you to see me crying," he admitted.

"In that car, you said I didn't look bad. But I did. You were lying then."

"Sorry," Wayne replied. "I were trying to pull you through."

Cassie hesitated and sighed. "How do I know you're not lying now?"

Wayne walked back over the bridge and stood awkwardly in front of her. "I'm not. If you think I am, I'm out of here. So, it's up to you. What do you think?"

Cassie gazed into his face. "No," she said at last. "You're telling the truth."

"Good."

A sad smile came to Cassie's war-torn face. "I guess I'll have to learn to forget, even though you'll be a constant reminder."

Wayne shrugged. "Suppose you will." Then he beamed mischievously at her.